# ZHOEL

---

## ALL I WANT FOR CHRISTMAS IS AN ALIEN

### KIRENAI FATED MATES (INTERGALACTIC DATING AGENCY)

### TAMSIN LEY

Twin Leaf Press

All characters in this book, be they supernatural, human, or something else entirely, are the product of the author's imagination. Any resemblance to actual people, situations, or events are entirely coincidental.

No part of this book may be reproduced, transmitted, or distributed in any form or by any means without explicit written permission from the author, with the exception of brief quotes for use in reviews, articles, or blogs. This book is licensed for your enjoyment only. Thank you a million zillion hearts and kisses for purchasing.

Cover by The Book Brander

Paperback version
ISBN-13: 979-8-89548-007-6
Copyright © 2024 Twin Leaf Press
All rights reserved.

Twin Leaf Press
PO Box 672255
Chugiak, AK 99567

# ACKNOWLEDGMENTS

To my VIP Club members Kathy G, Rebecca H, Katie, and Patricia Z: thank you for coming up with the awesome name for this book! It was hard coming up with a 'Zh' word that has holiday flavor, and I couldn't have done it without you.

To the rest of my wonderful VIP Club members: thank you for your incredible support, encouragement, and enthusiasm throughout this journey. Our interactions have meant the world to me as I wrote this book. Thank you for the inspiration!

To my amazing Jitters Critters critique partners: thank you for being my sounding board, my cheerleaders, and my voice of reason. Your honesty, your insight, and your belief in this story were invaluable.

To my readers: your love for these stories is what keeps me going. Thank you for purchasing my books, for spreading the word, and for always coming back for more. Because of you, I'm able to live out my dream of being a full-time author, and I can't thank you enough for being on this adventure with me.

XOXO, Tamsin

Zhoel closed his eyes on the silvery gleam of his ship's teleportation deck as the tingling thrum crawled over his body, feeling nervous about his first trip to Earth. He hoped his dark jeans and navy peacoat would help him look less alien, though his cobalt blue skin was an obvious giveaway. One misstep could ruin everything, and he had high hopes for this visit.

As the disorientation from travel faded, he drew in a deep breath of wintry air, sharp with the fragrance of tree resin and warm, sweet spice. He always enjoyed that first inhalation, that first primal insight of a strange new planet. Opening his eyes to muted daylight, he found himself staring directly into a pair of unblinking brown eyes.

"Kuzara," he swore, staggering back.

The being didn't move. *A statue.*

He let out a relieved breath and groped in his pocket for his Holographic Guidance Unit. The maps provided by the planetary database humans called "Goggle" had indicated these coordinates would be vacant, but as he craned his neck to the sky, a shoddily thatched roof stretched over his head. More carved wooden figures stood posed nearby, their painted eyes fixed adoringly on a small infant nestled in what appeared to be dried vegetation.

"Mommy, look, an angel!" a child's voice outside the shelter called.

Moving carefully around the statues, Zhoel emerged from the three-sided shelter onto a sidewalk where several humans wearing thick coats and scarves stood staring at him with their mouths open, each as still as the sculptures behind him. His empathic ability was too weak to fully grasp their emotions, but their body language radiated fear, curiosity, and what he thought might be outrage. His mouth went dry. *My arrival apparently interrupted something significant.*

Earth had only recently learned there were other species in the galaxy, and this was likely a first encounter for the people of Bloomington. He attempted a reassuring smile. "Forgive my intrusion."

A child in a bright pink coat with a white ruff of fur around the hood tugged on a woman's hand, her wide eyes reflecting the twinkling lights strung up on nearby structures. "I wanna talk to the angel!"

"He's not an angel, Claudia." The woman jerked the child back against the side of her long black coat. "He's an alien. And we don't talk to strangers." Pivoting, she towed the child behind her down the sidewalk.

In less than a heartbeat, the remaining townsfolk bolted as well, leaving him alone with the silent statues.

Zhoel cursed his weak Iki'i; any other Kirenai would've been able to read their feelings empathically and moderate the interaction. *Don't let your flaws interfere with your plan.* If humans dealt with each other without the use of an Iki'i, he could do it, too. Business contracts required numbers and logistics, not emotion. He only needed to find the

Carson Family Trucking office and negotiate a deal for surface transportation.

Males across the galaxy were clamoring to meet human females, but travel to Earth was strictly regulated by intergalactic law; the Intergalactic Dating Agency held the only permit. The IDA focused on marketing to Earth's dense population centers and usually transported females off-planet for massive dating events. Zhoel wanted to offer a more immersive dating experience with a focus on human culture, capitalizing on the unique charm of small communities like Bloomington. He'd endured headache-inducing bureaucracy—mostly caused by IDA interference—to secure a short-term business visa, and he had to make the most of his time here.

Zhoel shivered, the cold seeping through his clothing as fat white flakes of snow fell lightly from the overcast sky. He'd chosen his outfit based on a trendy human magazine, but now he wished he'd opted for a puffy jacket like the humans he'd just met. From somewhere far away, a song drifted toward him, his translator picking out the words, "Silent night, holy night..."

He looked in both directions along the empty street. A sagging layer of snow hid the nearby street sign, so he pulled out his Holographic Guidance Unit. Intergalactic law restricted surface mapping on Earth, which was still an underdeveloped and protected planet. Zhoel had luckily established a connection to the human's "Goggle" map database.

His teleporter was supposed to have placed him within walking distance of the trucking company, which, according to his contact, should be open for another hour and a half. The HGU's soft blue glow caught on falling snowflakes as he squinted at the flattened layout of the town. A glowing line showed a route between the closely set brick buildings.

Zhoel pulled the collar of his coat up, shoving his hands into his pockets as he walked. The snow was falling faster now, gathering on his shoulders and painting the sidewalk white. He turned a corner and spotted people moving between small shops and vehicles parked at the edge of the sidewalk, keeping their heads down against the increasing snowfall.

Moving forward cautiously and keeping his distance, he took in his surroundings. His arrival had already surprised a few locals, and the last thing he wanted was to accidentally offend more townsfolk.

On either side of the road, glittering circles of greenery dotted with bows and baubles hung from lamp posts. Small lights twinkled from windows, awnings, and even the bare branches of trees. He paused at a window display of a pointed evergreen that glittered with tinsel, its lower branches hovering over brightly wrapped boxes like a *damtal* hen with her chicks. Another store emitted a delightful smell that reminded him of sticky *kazhitsu* buns. Many businesses were playing festive music, and everywhere he looked there were fascinating displays of colored light. The diversity of human languages and traditions on Earth were still under documentation, but it seemed something important was happening in this town. *This is probably an experience my clients would enjoy.*

He turned another corner, still following the route on his HGU, and paused in front of a large window stenciled with enormous sparkly silver snowflakes. Inside, a harried-looking female tried to coax a crying toddler to sit on the lap of a rotund man with a white beard and red suit. The child's wails echoed through the glass.

Recalling the infant in the display of statues, Zhoel

pressed his face closer, slightly worried. *Is this some sort of ritualistic offering?*

"Please, sweetie, just one picture with Santa for Grandma," the woman pleaded, her voice nearly drowned out by the child's screeching cries.

Not an offering, then, but possibly a ritual. Perhaps a coming of age or consecration of some kind.

A gust of wind nipped at his exposed skin, and he turned away from the shop, boots plowing a trail through the snow now covering his toes. He'd walked for at least fifteen more minutes before he realized he was once again looking into the window where the plump, red-coated man had sat. The chair was now vacant.

Frowning, he stared at his HGU. *It's sending me in circles.*

"Kuzara," he swore, and stepped into an alleyway out of sight of any passersby. He thumbed the device, checking the status of the human map database, and got a message that his "app was up to date." *This is a perfect example of why my clients will pay top dollar for my services.* Once he'd partnered with a human company, they'd handle these types of logistics so none of his clients would get lost or stranded. *Especially in the middle of a blizzard.*

Zhoel straightened his shoulders and shoved his HGU back into his pocket. Time to get directions in the old-fashioned way—by asking.

He stepped back onto the sidewalk, glancing in both directions. The sky had darkened to pewter, and the lamp posts along the street had flickered on, casting cones of yellow light downward through the accumulating snow. There were no humans in sight, but the sound of singing drifted from somewhere nearby. He followed the music, rounding a corner to discover a town square dominated by an enormous glittering tree. A group of singers stood near the base belting out, "Oh, Christmas tree!" as if in worship of the towering monolith.

Reluctant to interrupt their ceremony, Zhoel waited, scanning the nearby storefronts for signs of the trucking office. The light inside one store went out, then another.

*Bong.* A bell tolled once across the square.

The song concluded, and the singers moved away, laughing and talking. Zhoel followed at a discreet distance, straining his feeble empathic senses to select which human might be most willing to speak with an alien. He didn't like to rely on his Iki'i, but after the fiasco with the statues, he needed any edge he could get. Yet he couldn't get a firm grasp on any one person, the wisps of their emotions dissolving like melting snowflakes.

The singers ducked into one of the parked vehicles along the street.

*They're leaving.* Frantic, Zhoel darted forward, boots slipping on a patch of ice. He caught himself against a nearby bench, regaining his balance in time to see the vehicle speeding away, its glowing red taillights quickly swallowed by falling snow.

Berating himself, he turned back toward the shops, searching for someone else to give him directions. The sidewalks appeared deserted, and more shop lights had dimmed, leaving the square illuminated only by the twinkling pinpricks of light covering the massive tree.

Desperate and getting colder by the second, Zhoel headed toward a store that still appeared occupied. Warm light flickered between cluttered stacks of books in the window, and a faded sign over the door read Brooke's Books. As he reached for the door handle, a woman emerged, her arms laden with a swaying pile of hardbacks. Her head was turned back over her shoulder, still engaged in a conversation with someone inside the shop.

"Thanks for staying, Brooke! These will be perfect for the—Oh!" She exhaled as she collided directly into Zhoel's chest.

The pile of books teetered dangerously, and he righted them just before they slipped from her grasp. Her pink-flushed cheeks deepened in color as she stared up at him with warm hazel eyes. A tangle of chestnut hair spilled out from beneath her yellow knit cap.

His Iki'i spiked with unusually strong arousal. *Hers? Or mine?* She was strikingly lovely, and his mating rod stirred to attention, making his heart race. He'd never had such an acute reaction to a female. They stood with their eyes locked in a moment that stretched and stalled under the softly falling snow.

Then a horn beeped, making the woman startle.

"Excuse me," she said in a breathy voice that made his insides flip-flop. She ducked past him and climbed into a waiting vehicle with a man in a baseball cap at the wheel.

*Husband?* Jealousy flared briefly before Zhoel shook his head. His task was to arrange a business deal, not find a mate, and he had limited time to do it. Yet he stood and watched the vehicle's tail lights retreat before he turned back to the shop.

As he entered, a cozy blanket of warm air embraced him, along with the dry aroma of old paper and ink. The shop's interior held towering shelves crammed full of physical books. More volumes were stacked haphazardly on tables and floor, like a small city of skyscrapers waiting to topple. A middle-aged woman with graying hair glanced up from where she stood behind a counter, her mouth dropping open. An orange cat slept lazily on a pile of cushions near the register.

"You're..." the woman gulped and stammered. "I'm sorry, but we're about to close."

"I'm not here to buy anything," Zhoel said, bringing out his HGU. Its blue light gleamed like ice under the shop's warm glow. "I need directions, please. It seems 'Goggle' isn't as accurate as I require."

The woman's eyes widened at the device, but she chuckled softly. "You mean Google? Yes, their map of Bloomington wasn't any good even when it was up to date. Where are you trying to go?"

"Carson Family Trucking."

The proprietor's brow furrowed. "Really? That was Lila Carson you just bumped into. She basically runs the business."

He turned, as if expecting the alluring woman to reappear in the doorway at her name. His heart was beating slightly too fast. That was the person he was supposed to meet? The idea of working closely with the hazel-eyed woman made him giddy. "She has already departed the area. Can you please tell me how to reach her?"

The woman scratched her jaw. "Their office closes up early this time of year. They won't open again until Monday."

His chest tightened. "I'm on a limited time travel visa. I can't wait until Monday." Zhoel turned back to her. "Can you provide me directions to her domicile?"

"Her house?" The woman's gray eyebrows shot up, and she shook her head. "I don't think that's a good idea."

He'd read all the IDA's pamphlets, and recalled one section mentioning that humans liked to give and receive "tips" for services rendered, so he rummaged in his pocket, producing several slips of human money he'd brought for just this reason. "I very much appreciate your assistance."

"Money's not the issue." She crossed her arms, her expression darkening. "I'm just not in the habit of directing strange alien men to the homes of young women."

Zhoel couldn't misread the wariness now radiating off the woman, regardless of his faulty Iki'i. "My apologies if I offended," he said, stuffing the bills back into his pocket. "I've been corresponding with another representative from Carson Trucking—someone named Pearl. Perhaps you could direct me to find them?"

"Pearl is Lila's grandma."

He narrowed one eye hopefully. "I suppose directing me to her home is no better than directing me to Lila's."

She laughed, her features softening slightly. "Pearl and Lila live together. Tell you what—why don't I give Pearl a call and see what she says?"

The woman removed a rectangular device from her pocket and, within a few minutes, was speaking to someone. He caught fragments of an elderly woman's voice, including the word dating and Lila. Finally, the bookstore proprietor pocketed the device, a humorous glint now lighting her eyes.

"Well, Pearl says to send you on over. If you give me a few minutes to close up, I'll give you a ride."

"I am deeply grateful for your help." Zhoel bowed, relieved he'd be speaking with Pearl about his business; if he had to make a deal with an alluring woman like Lila, he'd never be able to focus.

2

Lila put a steadying hand on the dashboard as her brother fishtailed his pickup around the corner. "I'm telling you, it was a real live alien back there!"

Tom sat hunched over the steering wheel, eyes squinting against the blowing snow. "Looked human to me."

"You couldn't see him through the snow. His skin was bright blue," she insisted as the old truck rattled along the street toward home.

"You sure he wasn't just blue from the cold?"

She hit her brother's arm with the back of her hand. "Yes. Human skin can't get that blue."

Other than his blue skin, the alien she'd just bumped into had seemed as human as any other man she'd met. Polite, even, helping her keep her stack of books from falling. He'd felt like a solid brick wall when she'd collided into him, and she'd been near enough to smell the damp wool of his peacoat mixed with a hint of maleness that hadn't struck her as alien at all.

Her thoughts drifted to a documentary she'd watched surreptitiously in her bedroom after her parents and Nana had gone to sleep. It had been about the more intimate aspects of the aliens, extolling their virtues as lovers. Most likely a bit of alien propaganda, but she'd indulged herself by watching it several times. After seeing an alien up close, she could believe the documentary might be true. She imagined what the tall, muscular alien might look like naked, and a little thrill raced through her. Pressing her thighs together, she stared at the snow pelting the windshield to avoid looking at her brother. *It might be best to change the subject.*

"Speaking of cold, why is your heater still broken?" She tugged her coat tighter around her chest; her toes felt like popsicles in the ballet flats she'd worn to work. "You'd think a mechanic would keep his own truck repaired."

He cut her a snide glance. "And you'd think a thirty-two-year-old woman would be smart enough to wear boots this time of year."

Lila scowled. "That's easy for you to say. You work in back. I'm in the front office. I have to look professional."

"You could just change into your fancy shoes when you get there. Besides, when's the last time a client walked in and wanted to chat face-to-face?"

Sweat prickled her skin despite the cold air blowing over the dash. Clients were few and far between these days, even at the height of the Christmas season. The family trucking business wasn't just struggling; it was on life support. Bills were piling up faster than the snow outside, and if something didn't change soon, they'd be buried under them. Lila glowered at the giant inflatable Santa waving from the Keller's yard as they passed. "We're a trucking company that closes over Christmas. How stupid is that? I had to do some really creative bookkeeping to pay our invoices this month. Did you—"

"Whoa, whoa," Tom cut her off, braking hard enough at a stop sign to rattle the toolbox in the back seat. "Mom's rule, remember? No business talk during the holidays." He half-slid into the empty intersection before gunning it again.

Lila bit her lip, remembering the Christmas five years ago when Dad had suffered a near-fatal heart attack. The doctors had blamed it on stress, and the entire family had spent that holiday season in the hospital, praying he'd pull through. Mom had made the no-business-talk rule right then and there, and insisted on closing the company every Christmas since. Lila understood why, but it didn't make their current situation any less dire.

"Slow down," she complained, grateful at least the truck's seatbelts weren't broken. "There could be kids playing out here. And regardless of Mom's rule, we can't ignore reality simply because it's Christmas."

"Just wait until after the holidays, okay? There's nothing we can do right now, anyway."

Lila leaned her head against the cold window, watching the snow swirl in the headlights. "We're going to lose everything Grandpa worked so hard to build."

"I'll talk to Mom and Dad with you after Christmas, I promise. We'll figure something out. I don't want the business to go under any more than you do."

"You sure don't act like it," she grumbled as the Carson family house came into view, a two-story red brick structure with white trim and a pair of dormer windows. White Christmas lights edged the rooftop and outlined every window, with more coiled up the posts of the wrap-around porch. Giant candy canes lined the walkway, and a team of glowing reindeer appeared to be pulling Santa's sleigh across the front yard.

"Looks like Mom put Dad to work today," Tom said, pulling into the driveway. "The house looks great." He set the truck to park but left the engine running.

"Aren't you coming inside?" Lila asked, unbuckling her seatbelt. "Sara and the kids are supposed to be here."

"Naw. I have a date with Simone."

She raised an eyebrow at him. "That's the third night

this week. Are things getting serious between you two?"

His face flushed, and he rubbed the back of his neck. "I dunno. Think Mom would mind if I invited Simone to join us for Christmas?"

Lila grinned, though a small pang filled her heart. Her baby brother was in love, which meant she was the last sibling without a partner. "Are you kidding?" She gathered her books and reached for the door handle. "Mom and Dad would be thrilled if you invite Simone. They'd probably start planning your wedding the minute she walks through the door."

"Whoa, let's not get ahead of ourselves," Tom laughed, but Lila could tell he was pleased. "Tell Sara and the kids I'll see them at the carnival tomorrow."

"See you then." Lila hopped out and shut the door with a thud, wet snow leaking along the edges of her shoes. She trudged to the front door as Tom's truck tires skidded out of the driveway back into the street. Not for the first time, she yearned for a house of her own. Living with Nana and her parents saved money, and she was trying to save up for her dream trip to France. *Or not.* Her latest creative bookkeeping involved funneling her savings back into the trucking company accounts to pay the bills.

She rescued a tiny glove she spotted half-buried in the snow next to the steps before stomping up onto the porch. Her sister had her hands full with three kids, and for the next two weeks, the Carson house would be full of joyful chaos. Lila tucked the books inside her coat so the kids wouldn't spot the gifts, and opened the door.

Warmth rolled out into the night air, the scent of pot roast and potatoes mingling with the sweet aroma of butter and vanilla from Mom's sugar cookies. As expected, the entryway was cluttered with small boots and coats, and the chatter of children's voices nearly drowned out the Christmas carols belting from the living room audio system.

Lila closed the door and quickly tucked the kids' books onto a shelf in the front closet before shrugging off her jacket and hanging it on an overcrowded hook. Kicking off her damp flats, she slipped her feet into a pair of fuzzy slippers and headed to the living room.

Mom and Nana Pearl were bustling about, stringing

lights and hanging ornaments, while Sara's children darted around like hyperactive elves.

"Josh! Leave the cat alone or you'll get scratched!" Sara hollered from the rocking chair where she sat nursing her new baby. Wisps of dark hair were escaping her ponytail as her tired eyes met Lila's. "Hi Sis."

"Hi Sara." Lila swooped Josh into a hug, freeing the cat to dart underneath the sofa; Whiskers hated everyone except Dad, yet insisted on remaining underfoot anytime people were around. Lila pressed a solid kiss to her four-year-old nephew's soft chubby cheek. "Hey, kiddo."

Josh squeezed her hard around the neck, then squirmed to get down and join his younger sister Emily pushing toy cars across the carpet.

Lila grabbed her favorite ratty cardigan from the back of the sofa and stuffed her arms into its fuzzy embrace, noting Dad's empty recliner. "Dad's not home yet?"

"He's on his way," Mom said. A jaunty elf hat with tiny bells on the ends covered her stylish bob, jangling as Mom rummaged through a box of decorations. "He got a late start today after helping with the yard ornaments." Dad had retired from long-hauling, but he still drove a regular delivery route for several restaurants in nearby towns.

Nana Pearl looked up from where she was detangling a string of lights. Arthritis gnarled her knuckles, and her hair was white as the falling snow, but her vibrant spirit defied her age. "Why don't you put on something besides that old sweater, Lila?"

Lila frowned. Nana had knitted her this sweater years ago. "No way. I love this sweater."

Planting a kiss on Nana's forehead, she popped into the kitchen to grab a sugar cookie. The pot roast simmered gently in the crock pot, and she lifted the lid, releasing a fragrant burst of steam. Poking a potato, she checked its readiness. Almost done. Replacing the lid, she contemplated another cookie when the doorbell chimed a perky rendition of Jingle Bells.

She headed back to the living room to see Mom peering through the window into the thickly falling snow. "Is that Aunt Maggie? She knows she doesn't need to ring."

"I'll get it," Nana Pearl said, already hobbling toward the entryway. "Lila, take off that sweater."

Josh and Emily raced ahead of her. "I'll get it!" "I'll get it!"

Mom put a hand on her hip, watching Nana suspiciously. "Did she invite the mailman to dinner again?"

"Let her have her crush," Lila said with a smile. Nana had recently been talking about dating, and though the mailman was at least fifteen years her junior, Lila thought she'd detected a few sparks between them. "You always make plenty of food."

Sara had finished nursing the baby, and Lila held out her hands to take the newborn.

"Thanks," Sara said, passing her daughter over.

Lila inhaled her sweet baby scent and looked down at her newest niece. The baby's eyes were closed, soft lashes dark against pudgy cheeks, a tiny fist curled below her chin. "God, I love that new baby smell."

Sara wiped a splotch of spit-up milk from her shirt. "Easy for you to say."

"Where's Greg?" Lila asked, looking around for her brother-in-law,

A pained look crossed her sister's face. "You know. Working."

Lila frowned, feeling bad for her sister. Where Lila dreamed of travel, Sara had always dreamed of white picket fences and laughing children. *At least she got part of her dream.* Lila was stuck here in Bloomington, keeping the business afloat while her ex-fiancé explored the world without her. She'd ended her engagement with Craig after months of him complaining she never had time for him. It hadn't been fair to keep him tethered.

Josh and Emily's high-pitched giggles filled the air, and Lila glanced toward the foyer as they scurried back into the living room. Her jaw dropped. Standing at the entrance was a tall, blue-skinned man clad in a dark peacoat.

No, not a man. An alien.

*The* alien.

"Everyone, this is Zhoel," Nana Pearl announced gleefully, her eyes homing in on Lila. "He's staying for dinner."

"He's blue!" Josh crowed, his pudgy face scrunched up in delight.

"Yes, he is," Sara answered warily, standing and pushing the kids behind her.

"What is going on?" Mom demanded, the bells on her hat jangling as she looked from Nana to the newcomer.

Lila swallowed, her mouth suddenly dry. The alien was even more handsome than she remembered, his cobalt blue skin and close-cropped midnight blue hair glistening with melting snowflakes. His eyes were a mesmerizing shade of deep violet and were focused on her as if she was the only person in the room.

Nana took Zhoel's arm and tottered forward. "This is my daughter, Diane, my oldest granddaughter, Sara, and this lovely young lady here is Lila, the one you're here to see."

"Me?" Lila squeaked, pulse thundering in her ears.

"Thank you for agreeing to meet with me," Zhoel said in a voice as rich as Belgian chocolate. His attention flickered to the baby, then back to Lila's face, an unspoken question in his eyes.

Mom cleared her throat, removing her festive hat

and smoothing her hair back into place. "I don't understand. What is he doing here?"

"I told you—his name is Zhoel. He's Lila's date."

*Oh, no.* Lila tore her gaze away from the alien's handsome features and muscular build. Nana Pearl was at her matchmaking shenanigans again. "Nana, you need to ask before you arrange a date for me."

"Especially with blue guys," muttered Sara under her breath, extracting the infant from Lila's arms.

"I told you to change out of that sweater," Nana whispered loud enough for everyone to hear.

Lila's face heated as she realized she must look like a complete frump, but she pulled the sweater resolutely across her chest. *Who cares?* She didn't have time for dating. She smiled tightly at the alien. "I'm afraid there's been a misunderstanding."

His brows drew together in confusion. "Will you not at least listen to my proposal?"

*Proposal?* She'd heard these aliens moved fast, but...

Mom spoke before she could respond. "I don't mean to be rude, but Aunt Maggie and Uncle Rich already invited themselves over to see Sara and the kids. I'm not sure I made enough—"

"We have plenty to eat, Diane," Nana Pearl said, her eyes suddenly steely. "And I invited him. He's staying."

Mom's cheeks flushed a deep rose as she eyed Zhoel warily. "Can he even eat our food?"

Despite the circumstances, Lila felt bad for the guy, and he definitely didn't deserve her mother's rudeness. "Of course he can eat human food, Mom. And he can hear you, you know."

Zhoel met her gaze with a smile hot enough to toast marshmallows. "You are correct, Lila. My nutritional requirements are quite compatible with your Earth food."

The way he said her name sent a flood of heat up Lila's neck and across her cheeks as she recalled the other, more intimate ways Kirenai aliens were rumored to be compatible.

Zhoel turned back to Mom and bowed his head politely. "But I don't mean to intrude. I can wait outside until after you've finished your meal to speak with Lila."

"Don't be ridiculous!" Nana Pearl grabbed his hand and pulled him into the living room. "You're staying for dinner. Lila, why don't you show Zhoel to the dining room?"

Knowing Nana would not back down, Lila motioned for him to follow her. As she led Zhoel down the hall, she was acutely aware of the way his eyes followed her every move. She couldn't decide what worried her more—that this alien was here with romantic intent, or that a tiny part of her was tempted to see where that intent might take them.

3

Zhoel was still reeling slightly from the way Pearl Carson had whisked him into the house, saying something about arriving in time for dinner. He knew humans often conducted business dealings over a meal, so he'd agreed. Plus, the experience would help him inform his clients about what to expect if/when humans opened their homes to them. But he didn't understand the tension thrumming across his Iki'i from members of the family. Lila was the only one who didn't vibrate with distrust. Instead, mixed in with the threads of her curiosity, he thought he felt... desire?

He'd never felt such an intense attraction toward anyone, through his Iki'i or otherwise. Her chestnut-brown hair swayed with each step as she led him down a hallway, and he yearned to slide his fingers through those silky strands. To glide his palms over the lovely curve of her hips as they swayed ahead of him...

He clenched his fists at his sides, cutting off the direction of his thoughts. He'd interpreted the sensations from his Iki'i wrong too many times before, including one mistake that had cost his father an important client. And despite the unusually intense emotions he received from Lila, he would not pursue her unless she actively invited his attention.

Lila led him to a room with a massive table draped in a red cloth and surrounded by a dozen wooden chairs. She glanced over her shoulder at him, her hazel eyes catching the light in a way that made him suck in a breath. "Welcome to the Carson family dining room," she said, moving toward a cabinet near a set of half-doors with slatted louvers that obscured the room beyond. "Can I pour you a drink?"

"Yes, thank you." He surveyed the table, set with perfectly arranged plates painted with green and red patterns of flora. Twinkling lights outlined the window frames, casting a pale glow against the snow-dusted panes. "I've never been inside a human's home. This is delightful."

She chuckled. "It doesn't normally look this way. Mom starts decorating the day after Thanksgiving and just keeps adding more throughout the month of December. You should see the house on Christmas morning."

Garlands interspersed with red and gold ornaments draped haphazardly along the top of a glass curio cabinet holding small statuettes, and beside it a sideboard held a fan-like arrangement of flowers, bows, and baubles. It reminded Zhoel of the Florenk celebrations on his mother's planet, where they would arrange B'laan fruit in elaborate patterns during festivals. The sight brought a surge of nostalgic delight.

"Does this Christmas morning happen soon?" He had briefly scanned Earth's Internet for holiday dates, but it seemed humans were celebrating something almost every day of the year, and he hadn't been able to make sense of the data. "I would be interested in experiencing your celebration."

Lila's shoulders stiffened. "Not for a few days."

He swallowed, uncertain what his Iki'i was sensing. *Did I overstep?*

Before he could frame the question, Pearl entered and pulled out a chair. "Sit here, Zhoel, so you'll be next to Lila. I'll get you a plate."

He sat, feeling awkward at being the only one at the table, but perhaps this was another custom he was not aware of. "Thank you."

The sound of heavy boots stomping off snow echoed through the house, followed by a booming voice. "I'm home! Had to stop and dig these two out of a snowbank."

"Grampa!" the children squealed from the other room, followed by the jumbled sound of females exchanging excited greetings.

"What is your mother feeding you two?" the deeper voice continued. "I can't believe how big—" He cut off, followed by indistinguishable muttering.

A moment later, a man with salt-and-pepper hair and a well-trimmed beard entered the dining room, a child wriggling in each arm. Behind him trailed another male wearing a plaid shirt and a female with short brown hair and deep laugh lines around her eyes.

"Wow," the woman said, an impish grin lighting her face. "This is going to be an interesting dinner."

Pearl clapped her hands together, looking immensely pleased with herself. "Zhoel contacted me about something called a dating app. I couldn't get the thing to work on my phone, but he mentioned being interested in transportation and travel, so I emailed him back to set up a date for Lila. She likes to travel."

"Nana!" Lila gasped. "You signed me up for a dating app?"

"Well, you've turned down everyone else I suggested."

Lila shot him an apologetic look. "I'm so sorry, but I'm really not interested in romance right now."

A sinking feeling filled Zhoel, not just over Lila's confessed lack of interest in him, but in his hope of making a deal with the Carson's company. This was all a misunderstanding. Pearl was trying to play matchmaker for her granddaughter and thought he'd been requesting a date.

He cleared his throat. "Actually, my dating app is—"

But his explanation was cut short as Pearl excitedly began introductions. "Zhoel, this is my son, Adam." She gestured to the bearded man. "And this is Lila's Aunt Maggie and Uncle Richard."

Adam thrust out a hand.

Deciding the best way to handle the entire fiasco was to play along until he could politely extricate himself, Zhoel mimicked Adam's gesture as he'd been told was customary for humans. "Good to meet you."

Adam clasped his hand and shook it firmly, his calloused palm still chilly from being outside. "Likewise. Welcome."

The woman named Maggie took the seat next to Zhoel and leaned close. "Lila's a lucky girl. I've heard about you blue aliens and your extra-terrestrial... ahem... abilities."

"Aunt Maggie, stop," Lila choked out, her embarrassment rippling across his Iki'i like a herd of tiny feet. She set a glass of golden liquid near his plate and sat down next to him.

"Abilities?" Zhoel repeated. Kirenai were strong and resilient, but he got the feeling Maggie meant something else entirely.

Maggie raised an eyebrow, then gazed pointedly toward his lap.

"Hush, you two!" Lila's mom admonished from where she stood near one of the louvered doors, her features creased in alarm. "There are little ones present."

"Don't mind Diane. She's a prude," Aunt Maggie said and winked at Lila. "You can tell me about it later."

Lila shot to her feet, face flushed a deep scarlet. "Mom, let me help you with the mashed potatoes."

As they disappeared through a set of half doors, Zhoel returned his attention to the other family members, avoiding Aunt Maggie's gaze.

Adam quirked an eyebrow and shrugged as if to say, 'Welcome to the family,' before pulling out the chair at the head of the table. "Zhoel, why don't you tell us more about yourself? I met an alien once when I was in Tampa last year, but he was gray with wings, not blue like you. You look a lot more… human."

Needing to resettle his nerves, Zhoel took a sip from his glass, finding the beverage sweet and somewhat floral. "It sounds like you met a Khargal. I'm Kirenai. You can always distinguish us because of our blue skin."

"I heard Kirenai can make themselves look like any human they see," Maggie said. "Is that true?"

Zhoel shook his head, glancing at the others before answering to be sure Aunt Maggie wasn't going to get him into trouble. Reassured by their interested gazes, he said, "I can't look like a specific human, but I can change my shape."

The small boy bounced in his seat. "Show us!"

"Don't be rude, Josh," Sara said with a stern look.

"I don't mind." He once again made eye contact with Adam, and, after receiving a nod, held up his hand for the boy. His skin rippled and undulated, fingers shortening and curving inward to form a large pincer in place of his hand.

A gasp filled the room. "Well, I'll be," said Pearl.

Josh laughed with excitement while his younger sister squealed and buried her face in her mother's lap. Both Adam and Richard leaned closer, their eyes wide with fascinated curiosity.

"Thank you for showing us," Sara said with an edge to her voice, stroking her little girl's head to comfort her. "Now, please change it back. You're scaring my daughter."

"Emily's a big baby," said Josh, which elicited wails of angry indignation from his sister.

"My apologies." Zhoel quickly shifted his hand back to its human form. He flexed his fingers for Emily, proving that things were back to normal. Interacting with humans was more difficult than he'd imagined. He'd have to be sure to note that in his travel FAQs.

Lila and her mother returned from the kitchen carrying steaming dishes, and the savory aroma he'd noticed upon entering the house intensified.

"Here we go, everyone." Diane announced, placing a platter at the center of the table. It held a reddish-brown meat and some orange root vegetables. Lila added a dish of something fluffy and white with a crater of golden oil at the top plus a dish of thin green vegetables.

Zhoel's nostrils flared at the rich, mouth-watering aromas. Human food smelled unexpectedly delicious. Another experience his clients would love.

"Let's say grace," Diane commanded, sitting next to her husband and reaching for his hand.

Maggie grabbed Zhoel's hand, fingers kneading slightly as if checking to see that his flesh was solid.

On his other side, Lila hesitated, glancing at him from beneath her lashes before offering her hand. He took it, tingling with awareness as their palms met. Her skin was soft and warm as he skimmed his thumb across the backs of her knuckles. Her eyes widened, and she sucked in a soft breath before quickly lowering her chin to her chest.

His Iki'i was oscillating between desire and discomfort. *Can you blame her?* Her grandmother had mistaken his intent and set her up on a date without telling her. Perhaps her emotions would steady once he clarified the misunderstanding.

The rest of the family joined hands, forming a circle around the table, and Adam intoned a prayer. "We thank you, Lord, for this food we are about to receive. We welcome our guest tonight, and ask that his journey be blessed. Let us cherish this time together as family, and remember the love that binds us all. Amen."

"Amen," echoed throughout the room.

Touched to be included in the prayer, Zhoel added his own, "Amen," to the mix.

Lila quickly pulled her hand away and arranged her napkin across her lap, then reached for a serving spoon. "Is this your first time trying human food?"

"Yes," Zhoel said, watching her place a brown slab of what he believed was meat on his plate.

She pointed to the various items. "Pot roast, carrots, mashed potatoes, green beans."

Knowing she'd taken part in preparing the mashed potatoes, he sampled a bite, delighted by the rich, buttery flavor with a hint of earthy sweetness. "Delicious." He smiled at her, loving the slight rise of color in her cheeks at the compliment. He sampled the pot roast and carrot, finding them equally intriguing, and praised Lila's mother, which seemed to fluster her. She turned to help Josh cut bites of food while Sara helped Emily.

As the family ate, they chattered amongst themselves. Zhoel happily immersed himself in the feeling of family, enjoying a warm sense of belonging for the first time since his arrival. Then he remembered he wasn't actually here to enjoy himself. *It's time to get down to business.*

He looked around to be sure Pearl wasn't watching, then lowered his voice. "Lila, I believe your grandmother may have mistaken the reason for my visit. I'm starting up a new dating and travel app to bring aliens to small towns on Earth. I was hoping to discuss a partnership with your transportation company to handle surface logistics."

She blinked at him. "Wait. So you're not here to date me?"

He held up one hand, suddenly fearful she might be offended. "Don't misunderstand. I'm delighted and honored to spend time with you. I would definitely like to continue. However, I felt it was important to be honest about my original purpose here."

Lila burst out laughing, a delightful sound that reminded him of happa leaves swaying together in the sun. "I can't tell you how glad I am to hear that." She leaned closer, eyes alight with interest, then glanced toward her mother. "Please tell me more about your proposal, but keep your voice down. Mom doesn't like business talk during the holidays."

As they ate, Zhoel spoke enthusiastically about his vision for the app, his ideas for how it could weave together the experiences of Earth and alien cultures while fostering connections and understanding. He loved seeing Lila grow more excited with every description. "I want to offer tours that provide the experiences of eating unique foods, taking part in local activities, and interacting with humans in more natural settings. A way to find prospective mates that goes far beyond the more formal galas offered by the Intergalactic Dating Agency."

"That sounds amazing." Lila smiled wistfully. "But our trucks transport freight, not people. I don't think we can help you."

Zhoel scratched his ear. He'd apparently mistaken the word transportation to mean travel. But he truly wanted to work with Lila. "You are familiar with travel across the planet's surface, correct? What if I provide the appropriate vehicles?"

Her eyes lit with excitement once more. "I suppose our drivers could operate buses as easily as semis. And I would love to plan logistics for travel."

"What's this about driving buses?" Lila's father asked.

Diane rose abruptly, eyes flashing in anger. "Lila, are you talking about the business again?"

"Now, Diane—" Adam started at the same time Lila said, "We're on a date, Mom! We're talking about our interests."

Zhoel held his breath. Did Lila still consider this a date? Or was she only using that as an excuse to continue their discussion? Either way, he would help her in any way he could.

He turned to Diane with a warm smile. "Mrs. Carson, I assure you that Lila and I are just getting to know each other better. We both have a strong interest in travel and logistics, which naturally came up in our conversation."

Her expression softened slightly at his polite tone, though she still looked uncertain.

Nana Pearl chimed in. "Why don't you two continue your date in private in the den? The fire is so cozy this time of night."

Lila shot her grandmother a grateful look and stood, motioning for Zhoel to follow her. "That sounds great, Nana."

He rose from his chair, giving the family a polite nod, and followed Lila out of the dining room, his heart racing. *Negotiations or not, perhaps this just turned into an actual date after all.*

## 4

Embarrassed by her mother's rudeness, Lila led Zhoel from the dining room, her heart still pounding from the tension at the dinner table. She pushed open the door to the den, revealing shelves full of ratty paperbacks, several comfy chairs, and a gas fireplace. Only the Christmas lights around the window currently lit the room, and she hit the remote to turn on the fire. Its flames burst into life, casting dancing shadows across the bookcases. Mom's holiday mania hadn't fully reached here yet, and aside from the lights in the window, the room was unadorned.

Breathlessly aware of Zhoel's towering presence behind her, Lila gestured toward the rugged leather couch in front of the fireplace. "Please have a seat."

The firelight reflected lavender highlights off Zhoel's cobalt blue skin, emphasizing the cut of his jaw and the sensuous curve of his lips. Lila's breath caught as he moved gracefully toward the fireplace and plucked up a snow globe from among the family photos.

"What's this?" he asked, turning it over in his hands.

"A snow globe." Lila stepped closer to see which one he held. He smelled like cocoa butter and sandalwood, a scent that made her feel pleasantly at ease. "You shake it to make the 'snow' inside swirl around."

"Fascinating!" Zhoel turned it right side up, smiling as the glittering flakes drifted down among the miniaturized skyline of Chicago. "But why is it significant?"

"My dad used to bring them home from his trips, a representation of the places he'd been when he couldn't be here with us. That's why my mom goes all out with the decorations. I think she was trying to make up for his absence."

"Does he no longer take such trips?"

Lila shook her head. "No. He had a heart attack a few years ago. Since then, Mom insists he only drive short routes, which has been hard on the business…" Her complaints died on her tongue as she recalled that terrifying Christmas in the hospital, taking turns sleeping on the uncomfortable pull-out chair next to his bed, holding his hand, praying for him to get better while he drifted in and out of consciousness. She swallowed the lump in her throat. "But we're just happy to have him alive and home for the holidays."

"It sounds like his illness must have been difficult," Zhoel said softly.

"Yes. We still worry about him. It's why Mom is so insistent about not talking business, especially around the holidays and especially when Dad's around."

She reached out to take the snow globe back, fingers brushing against Zhoel's. A jolt of electricity seemed to pass between them, and her eyes lifted to find him staring at her.

"You are very lucky to have your family so near." His hand clasped hers gently around the snow globe. "I hope us working together can help ease your stress."

The look in Zhoel's eyes suggested that despite the date being merely a ruse, there could be more than just business between them.

Praying he couldn't sense the turmoil his touch had stirred within her, she placed the bauble back on the mantel. She let her gaze briefly sweep the other cityscapes dusted in snowy perfection before turning back. "What about your family? Do you see them often?"

A tightening around his eyes and mouth spoke of some deep-seated pain, but then he shrugged. "The universe is vast. I don't see them often." He settled onto the couch, draping one arm casually along the back. "Will you tell me more about Christmas? I saw several instances of rituals with young children while I was in town."

She laughed. "Rituals?"

"Yes. When I arrived, I found myself among statues that seemed to be offering reverence to an infant. And then there was a ritual with a man in a red suit I saw through a store window."

"Ah." Lila smiled and sat on the opposite end of the couch. "Christmas is… complicated. It's supposed to be a religious holiday celebrating the birth of Jesus Christ—that's probably the statues you saw, a Nativity scene. But the holiday has grown to include many non-religious traditions, too. The red-suited man you're describing is Santa Claus. Children ask him for gifts, which he leaves under a tree on Christmas morning."

"Fascinating. Do all humans observe this holiday?"

"No," she said. She'd never had to describe a holiday to an alien before—or anything to an alien, for that matter. "Not everyone believes in Jesus, or even celebrates Christmas. There are people who just observe the traditions of gift-giving and family time. Other people celebrate different religious holidays around the same time of year—Hanukkah and Kwanza, for instance—and some people don't observe any holiday at this time of year at all."

Zhoel's brow furrowed slightly. "Such diversity among human culture. It's remarkable. My clients would pay appreciable amounts to experience them all. I hope we can find a mutually beneficial way for our companies to work together."

Lila glanced toward the open doorway before leaning closer, her voice dropping to a whisper. "My family might be listening. We need to keep up the illusion of our date, remember?"

Understanding flickered in Zhoel's eyes, and he scooted closer, his hip bumping her leg on the couch. "Of course." His voice adopted a more playful lilt. "As I was saying, I would very much like to enjoy further experiences here on Earth with you."

His cocoa butter and sandalwood smell gave her the crazy desire to haul herself over his lap and straddle him where he sat. She wanted to give him some experiences, all right.

*Good Lord, what's wrong with me?* Did all aliens make human women want to do crazy things? She pulled a pillow onto her lap like a shield, fidgeting with its tassels as she tried to quell her nervous energy. "How did you get into the travel business, anyway?"

The playful light in Zhoel's violet eyes dimmed, his expression growing serious. He leaned back slightly, turning to stare at the dancing flames in the fireplace. "My parents own a chain of luxury hotels. Growing up, I never liked how the local hotel staff were treated like non-entities by the guests. They were just background scenery for the visitors. When

I… left home, I traveled a bit, enjoyed immersing myself in other cultures."

He rubbed his palms up and down his thighs, as though brushing off a memory before turning to smile at her. "I remember visiting this one planet, Korrax-5… it wasn't the most glamorous destination, not like the grandeur of Stratonis or the beaches of Maelara. But the inhabitants had a fascinating culture. Their lives revolved around light."

Entranced by the idea of traveling to alien worlds, Lila leaned forward, the pillow shield on her lap forgotten. "Around light? How?"

"Their days are extraordinarily long—something like a month of your Earth days—and they hold a procession at each dawn and dusk. They gather around these enormous crystal obelisks and sing. The notes start a vibration in the crystals that synchronize throughout the city. Simply amazing."

"God, I'd love to see that," Lila said, breathless at his description.

He smiled at her. "I'd love to show you. The best part was the way they brought me into the celebration. I sang with them, feeling the hum of their song from the soles of my feet to the roots of my hair. I still keep in touch with my friends there and want to create that type of experience all over the galaxy—a travel experience that prioritizes a genuine connection with other cultures and personal growth over superficial luxury."

"That's a wonderful goal," Lila said, genuinely impressed. She felt a familiar ache in her chest, one that always surfaced when she thought about the places she'd never seen. Now she could add other planets to her never-ending wish list. "I've always dreamed of traveling," she said, her voice barely above a whisper. "But between the family business and, well, life... I've never even left Bloomington."

"Never?" he asked, shock visible in his features.

Lila shook her head and smiled ruefully. "Pathetic, right? Thirty-two years old and I've never even seen the ocean." She fiddled with a loose thread on her cardigan, avoiding his gaze. "I even thought about getting my CDL so I could drive trucks like Dad, but I failed the test twice and nearly crashed our semi during practice, so I gave up."

Before her melancholy could drag her under completely, she shrugged. "But hey, Bloomington might be small, but we have lots of things to do here.

In fact, our annual Christmas Carnival is happening tomorrow. You should come."

Zhoel's eyes widened with interest. "I would enjoy seeing another aspect of human culture. And," he added, leaning closer, voice taking on a sultry note, "I find I quite enjoy your company."

She realized he was probably just saying it in case her family was listening, but she was enjoying his company, too. Perhaps he would stay in contact with her like he did with his friends on Korrax-5. *Or perhaps he can help get our business back on track and I can actually take a trip to the stars.* She let out a slow breath. "Maybe we could extend our... date for a few more days? To, you know, keep talking."

He nodded enthusiastically, but then grimaced. "There is one minor issue. I assumed our negotiations would conclude quickly. I don't have lodging. Perhaps you can help me arrange accommodations for the night?"

She wrangled her phone out of her back pocket, excited at the prospect of having another day or two with him. "I'm sure the Bloomington Bed and Breakfast has plenty of rooms available. Let me call them right now."

Her fingers trembled slightly as she dialed the number. *Zhoel wants to stay.* And she was pretty sure he was interested in more than just business with her. After Craig, she'd given up on romance—but a fling with an alien? Maybe.

"Hello, Bloomington Bed and Breakfast," a cheerful voice answered.

"Hi, Mrs. Hawkins," Lila said, recognizing the owner's voice. "This is Lila Carson. We have an unexpected guest in town, and I was wondering if you have a room available tonight?"

"Oh, I'm so sorry, dear. We're completely booked through the holidays. You know how busy it gets this time of year."

"Oh, okay. Thanks anyway, Mrs. Hawkins." She hung up with a sigh. "They don't have room."

Zhoel shook his head sadly. "Are there no other accommodations in the area?"

*This is a chance to prove you can handle logistics, Lila.* But the Bloomington B&B was the only one within a thirty-mile radius. She couldn't fail now, and truly wasn't ready for Zhoel to leave—for multiple reasons. Before she even realized what she was doing, she blurted, "We have a guest room here. Why don't you stay with us?"

Zhoel's eyebrows shot up, surprise etched across his cobalt features. "Are you certain? You seem to have many family members. I wouldn't want to impose."

"It's no imposition," Lila quickly assured him, suddenly giddy at the idea of an attractive alien sleeping just down the hall.

A slow smile spread across Zhoel's face, sending a flutter through Lila's stomach. "Then I gratefully accept your hospitality."

"Great. I'll go make up the bed for you."

She rose, feeling light on her feet. Then the realization of what she'd just done hit her like a snowball in the face. Mom had barely been civil to Zhoel during dinner. How was she going to react to him staying the night?

5

---

s Zhoel followed Lila up the stairs to a long hallway, he could barely contain his elation. He was about to stay in a human's home. The IDA would never offer such an immersive experience.

Lila stopped and gestured to a doorway. "This is the guest room." She pointed out another door farther down and cleared her throat. "I'm just down the hall. If you need anything, just come get me, okay?"

His heart skipped a beat. Was that an invitation? *No.* And even if it was, he couldn't indulge himself. He had only three days here before his visa expired. Getting side tracked by a romantic fling wasn't an option.

He smiled and dipped his head in gratitude. "Thank you. I'm sure I'll be fine."

She smiled back. "Have a good night."

Stepping into the room, he closed the door and turned to examine the warm wooden furniture and a bed with an intricately patterned quilt. *Fascinating.* Running a hand along the wooden dresser, he marveled at the rich grain beneath his fingertips.

When he moved to examine the quilt, a low growl made him pause. From the darkness under the bedframe, a pair of green eyes glared up at him.

An orange furred body emerged, back arched and long tail twitching. The creature bared its pointed teeth, ears laid back against its skull. *Hostile.* He'd encountered vermin several times during his travels, some more dangerous than others. He opened his Iki'i, projecting what he hoped would be interpreted as dominance, preparing to defend himself, when he spotted the collar around its neck.

"Ah." He relaxed. "You must be a family pet." Crouching down, he extended a hand. "I mean you no harm, small creature."

The creature gave him a haughty look, then stalked to the door and stood glaring at him, obviously demanding to be let out. *At least that's clear.* Zhoel opened the door a crack. The animal circled his ankle once, rubbing its sleek fur against him in gratitude before disappearing into the hallway.

Closing the door again, Zhoel sighed. If only he understood humans half as well. Stripping off his pants and shirt, he retired to the bed and fell into a restless slumber.

He wakened to a gentle knock at the door and sat bolt upright, reorienting himself to his surroundings. Morning sunlight streamed through the window, and a digital clock near the bed read eight thirteen.

"Zhoel?" Lila called softly. "Are you awake?"

He rose and smoothed down his midnight blue hair before opening the door. Lila stood there dressed in jeans and a thick boat neck sweater that showed off the delicate line of her collarbone. Her chestnut hair fell in luscious waves about her shoulders, making his fingers yearn to touch the silky locks. She stared at his bare chest and legs, throat moving visibly with a swallow before she dragged her attention up to his face.

"I hope you don't mind an early start," she said. "I thought we could grab coffee at a place nearby and talk without my family overhearing."

"Let me get dressed, then I'm at your disposal," he said. After dressing quickly, he followed her down the stairs to the front door.

She eyed his peacoat hanging on a nearby hook. "The cafe isn't far. I thought we'd walk. Is that your only jacket?"

"Yes. I did not anticipate extended exposure to weather."

"I think your shoulders are too big for any of Dad's coats." She dug in a basket near the door and produced a black fleece hat and gloves. Then she rummaged in the closet and pulled out a pair of heavy boots. "Here. See if these fit."

"Thank you." He secured the hat on his head and slid his feet into the boots, adjusting his appendages to better fit the contours. Lila put on a yellow knit hat and wrapped a matching checkered scarf around her delicate throat.

Outside, a pristine layer of snow glittered in the morning sun. The air was crisp, making him doubly glad for the gloves and hat. A neighbor across the way was pushing a loud machine that threw snow in a high arc, clearing a trail from the house to the street. During the night, the road and sidewalk had also been cleared, leaving a perfectly cut trail along the fronts of the houses. He'd never visited a location where the precipitation remained frozen before, and found the humans' maintenance of it delightful.

They walked side-by-side a few blocks until they reached a squat brick building with steamed-up windows. An elderly man exited, trailing a rich, slightly bitter aroma from the doorway. He stumbled, eyes going wide at the sight of Zhoel, then hurried to a car parked nearby.

Lila watched him with a frown, then leaned close to Zhoel. "Sorry. I didn't realize things might be awkward."

He shrugged. "It's normal. I'm an alien in a small town. I've had worse reactions on other planets."

She raised her eyebrows. "I'd love to hear more of your stories sometime."

Warming at the request, he nodded. "Of course."

Inside the cafe, people sat scattered among weathered wooden tables. Near the back wall, a glass counter full of pastries separated the seating area from the kitchen. A large brick fireplace against the wall exuded waves of heat, and the sweet scent of baked goods intermingled with the bitter, yet tantalizing aroma Zhoel had detected outside. The patrons' lively chatter dwindled to a halt as Lila looped her arm through his and marched up to the counter.

A perky barista stared openly at Zhoel, mouth open in shock. After a moment, she said, "Uh, what would you like to drink?"

He scanned the board above the counter with confusion. *Americano, Latte, Cappuccino, Frappe...* Turning to Lila he said, "Whatever you're having," making a mental note to figure out the differences later for his clients.

Lila quickly ordered two mochas and handed him a plate of pastries before leading him to a tiny round table near the front. She set down two steaming mugs of a creamy brown beverage before taking a seat. Most people had returned to their conversations, though the glances in his direction told him many of those conversations were likely about him.

Lila wrapped her fingers around her mug and leaned forward over the table. "I've been thinking about your proposal and have some great ideas for local vacation packages we could put together. The real problem is that Mom insists on reviewing all our contracts, and she's not only adamant about not discussing business over the holidays, she's not great about thinking outside the box. We need to make the concept irresistible to her."

"I see," Zhoel said, taking a small sip of the scalding, bitter-sweet mocha as he contemplated ways they might win Diane over. "You said your father drives short routes. Is the rest of your family involved as well?"

"Everyone but Sara. I handle the bookkeeping. My brother Tom's our mechanic, keeps the trucks in top shape. Uncle Rich and cousin Jake drive the long hauls. "

"Perhaps if we get the rest of your family in agreement, they can help convince your mother."

Lila nodded thoughtfully and picked up a pastry. "Worth a try. But we can't let Mom know we're discussing business behind her back."

Zhoel picked up the other pastry and took a bite. The soft texture melted against his tongue with a rich sweetness he wasn't certain he enjoyed. He set it back on the plate. "Then we have a plan. Who do you suggest we talk to first?"

Before she could answer, a short woman wearing glasses approached their table. "Excuse me, but could I get a picture with you?" she asked Zhoel.

He stood. This was a custom he'd read about; humans liked to use visual documentation to share their experiences collectively with other humans. "It would be my pleasure."

The woman handed a small flat device to a companion and stood next to Zhoel, beaming up at him.

Zhoel grinned and slipped an arm around her shoulders in a friendly gesture, mimicking what he had seen in human interactions. His pose elicited a chorus of "awws" from nearby tables.

Apparently emboldened, a petite woman with curly blonde hair approached. "Hey, Lila. Who's your friend?" She held a small bundle of green leaves and white berries tied with a red ribbon above her head. Giving him a playful grin, she asked, "Can I ask him to stand under the mistletoe with me?"

Lila's expression darkened, and Zhoel's Iki'i flickered with a wave of emotions from her—something sharp, almost like... jealousy?

"Not now, Ann," Lila said. "Can't you see we're busy?"

Curious about a new custom, Zhoel asked, "What is the significance of this mistletoe?"

"It's a holiday tradition." The blonde leaned forward until she was looking directly into his eyes, arm still overhead. "When two people stand under it, they're supposed to kiss. It's considered good luck."

He glanced at Lila in alarm. A public display of affection with a stranger? If he was going to kiss anyone, he wanted it to be Lila. He quickly rose, taking himself out of range of the mistletoe in her outstretched hand. "Thank you for the offer, but I'm only here to observe."

The woman's cheeks flushed. "Well, can't blame a girl for trying." She flicked the mistletoe onto the table, shrugged, and flounced back to her table.

He turned to Lila. "Did I handle that correctly?"

"You handled it perfectly. Ann thinks every man in Bloomington is in love with her." She rose, draining the last of her mocha with a satisfied sigh. "Are you done? We should get going."

He nodded and put on his hat. Before following her out, he picked up the mistletoe and tucked it into his pocket. He needed all the luck he could get.

They exited into the brisk air and walked down Main Street toward the sound of tinny music. Soon, a row of colorful booths came into view with a sign proclaiming "Bloomington Christmas Carnival" hanging overhead.

A booming voice called out from ahead, and a portly man in a bright red suit emerged from the crowd. "Ho ho ho!"

Lila leaned in close, her breath warm against Zhoel's ear. "Uh oh. Brace yourself. Mayor Gunderson is playing Santa again."

"Welcome to Bloomington! I heard we had an extraterrestrial visitor in the area!" The man took Zhoel's hand and enthusiastically pumped it up and down. What appeared to be artificial white facial hair obscured his mouth and chin. "What brings an interstellar traveler like yourself to our humble town?"

Zhoel hesitated, his eyes darting to Lila. Should they maintain the ruse of their "date," or reveal their true intentions? He didn't want to jeopardize their budding partnership, but lying to a government official seemed unwise.

Lila came to his rescue, her voice steady. "Zhoel is looking for ways to bring more alien visitors to Bloomington."

The mayor's eyes lit up. "Here?"

Zhoel nodded. "Yes, we believe Bloomington has much to offer visitors from across the galaxy."

"Yes, yes!" The mayor clasped his hands together in delight. "We'd be honored to host friends from far away. Oh, that could be our slogan! Friends from far away. What an exciting opportunity! We simply must discuss our options."

Zhoel nodded. Lila rolled her eyes good-naturedly, a smile playing at the corners of her lips.

"We've been talking about logistics and ground transportation," she said. "It would be great if the city could form a tourism committee."

A sudden thought struck Zhoel, and he clasped the mayor's shoulder in a friendly grip. "Perhaps you could discuss ideas with Lila's mother? I hear she reviews the contracts for the family business, and I'm sure she'd be interested in your input."

"Capital idea!" The mayor beamed. "I'll give her a call. Now, if you'll excuse me, I've got a pie-eating contest to judge!"

As the mayor bustled away, Zhoel grinned at Lila. "Do you think the mayor's enthusiasm might help convince your mother?"

Lila's hazel eyes sparkled with laughter. "Perhaps. Though he can be a bit of a flake." Her gaze lingered on him for a moment before she took his hand and tugged him toward the heart of the bustling activity. "Let's go see some of that human culture you've been dying to experience."

Despite the cold, Zhoel felt a giddy warmth infuse him with her touch. Following her between the booths, the dazzling colors, spicy sweet smells, and milling people celebrating the holiday almost overwhelmed his senses. Lila bought them both spiced hot cider that warmed his hands and delighted his tongue as they went from booth to booth. They tried on ridiculous holiday hats at one stall, and Lila insisted on purchasing a festive red hat with a fluffy white pom-pom for him. He played several interesting games of skill and chance, winning a game of ring toss.

Zhoel examined the prize curiously. It was a soft, fluffy creature with large, round eyes and floppy ears. "What is this supposed to be?"

"It's a stuffed rabbit," Lila explained, rubbing the soft ears and smiling. "You know, like the animal?"

"Ah, I see." Zhoel held it out to her. "Would you like it?"

Lila's cheeks flushed pink. "Oh, um, sure." She accepted the rabbit, hugging it to her chest and laughing softly. "You're the first guy to win a carnival prize for me. Thanks." Then she pointed to a towering upright wheel with seats attached to its outer rim. "Want to ride the Ferris wheel?"

Zhoel hesitated. "Is it safe?"

Lila laughed, a warm sound that made Zhoel's skin tingle. "You just flew here in a spaceship and you're worried about a carnival ride?" She grabbed his hand. "Come on, this'll be fun."

They settled into a swinging seat and waited patiently for the car to ascend. He stared upward at the machinery and gears. Several lights along the struts appeared to be burned out, and the scent of oil drifted to him through the crisp winter air.

The Ferris wheel carried them to the top, and the carriage paused, swaying gently in the breeze. The town below was a winter wonderland, a patchwork of twinkling lights and snow-dusted rooftops, but Zhoel found it difficult to tear his gaze away from Lila. She shivered, gripping the stuffed animal tightly.

"Are you cold?" Zhoel raised an arm, offering his warmth.

"Thank you," she murmured and scooted closer.

His Iki'i thrilled at her nearness. It might be his imagination, but he felt as if his power was stronger, more confident around her.

She lifted her chin, looking up at him, her body full of nervous energy. *Does she want me to kiss her?* He thought about the mistletoe in his pocket and almost reached for it. But something held him back, a fear that his Iki'i was wrong, that one faulty move might shatter the connection growing between them. Then the Ferris wheel jolted into motion again, ending the moment.

When they finally stepped off the ride, Lila moved ahead through the crowd, and Zhoel felt a pang of disappointment, as if something important had just slipped through his fingers.

Suddenly, a man in a black coat and baseball cap surged forward, reaching out as if to grab Lila. Zhoel's instincts roared to life, and he blocked the man's arm, ready to defend her.

"Whoa there," the man said, jerking his hand back and scowling. He glared at Zhoel.

Lila turned. "Tom!"

"I talked to Sara this morning, and she told me about last night," Tom said, speaking to Lila but looking at Zhoel. "You're really dating an alien?"

A pretty woman standing next to the man elbowed him sharply. "Tom! Don't be rude." She turned to Zhoel with a warm smile. "It's nice to meet you. My name's Simone. Welcome to Bloomington."

Lila sighed. "Zhoel, this is my brother Tom and his girlfriend. This is Zhoel, you two. And yes, he's my date."

*Brother*. Tom was Lila's brother. Zhoel relaxed, determined to make a good impression.

"It's a pleasure to meet you both," he said. "Lila has told me so much about your family. I feel like I know you already. I understand you're the mechanic who keeps the Carson fleet running smoothly?"

Tom's scowl relaxed, but his shoulders remained rigid. "Yeah, that's right."

"I find Earth's ground transportation fascinating, especially the use of combustion engines. Perhaps you could tell me more about it sometime?" Zhoel asked, trying to open an opportunity for additional discussion.

Tom shrugged noncommittally. "If you're interested."

"Tom and I were heading to the skating pond," said Simone. "You should join us."

Lila looped her arm through Zhoel's. "You up for a real cultural immersion?"

Zhoel smiled, the prospect of another new experience—and more time with Lila—making his heart race. "I'd like nothing better."

A muscle in Tom's jaw twitched, his gaze on their looped arms. It seemed he was about to say something, but Lila shot her brother a warning look and he turned and stalked away. As they followed, Zhoel couldn't shake the feeling that winning over Lila and her family might be more challenging than he'd anticipated.

ila rented two pairs of skates from the small shack near the skating pond and led Zhoel to the benches where Tom and Simone were already lacing up. Smoke wafted from a warming barrel where several skaters stood clustered, hands out to catch the heat, and classic Christmas tunes filled the air, mixing with the laughter of children and the scrape of blades on ice.

"Here." She handed Zhoel his skates. "Try these on."

His blue skin seemed more brilliant under the soft glow of Christmas lights suspended from poles around the rink, and Lila was surprised to notice a sexy dusting of five-o'clock shadow along his jaw. Had that been there before?

Zhoel inspected the thin blades. "These are to glide on the ice?"

"Yes," she said, bending to put on her own skates. "Don't worry. I'll show you what to do."

Tom stood in front of their bench with his arms crossed, a skeptical twist to his lips. "You sure he's up for this? What if he falls and breaks a bone or something? I don't think our clinic knows how to fix aliens."

A flicker of irritation went through Lila at her brother's snarky tone. "He'll be fine, Tom." She looked at Zhoel. "Ignore him. You'll be fine."

Amusement flickered in Zhoel's eyes, and he looked around at the townsfolk moving across the ice with varying degrees of skill. "Don't worry. I'm a quick learner."

She smiled back, then leaned in to assist him with his laces while Tom and Simone joined the flow of other skaters on the rink. Once they were all laced up, she stood and offered Zhoel a hand to help him rise, bracing her legs to maintain her balance. She hadn't skated since last Christmas and hoped she didn't embarrass herself today.

Zhoel wobbled as he acclimated to standing on the thin blades. "Whoa." He gripped her hand more tightly. "This is… different."

His touch was innocent, but still sent flutters of awareness through her. She smiled up at him. "It takes some getting used to."

She led him to the edge of the pond. "Just keep your knees slightly bent and push off with one foot, then the other."

Zhoel's first few steps were shaky, his arms flailing as he tried to find his balance, but within a few minutes, he released her hand and took a few strides on his own. They completed a circuit around the rink, his movements becoming ever smoother and more controlled. *He really is a fast learner.*

Lila decided to show off a little, grinning as she turned around and skated backward. Although he no longer seemed to need her help, she held out her hands, enjoying his firm but gentle grip as she guided him forward. The music switched to a lively rendition of *Jingle Bell Rock* and she swayed her hips playfully in time to the beat.

His eyes gleamed with admiration, and he modified

his strides to match hers. "Skating is exhilarating. I can see why humans enjoy it."

"You're doing great," she said as a group of townsfolk skated past, their reactions varying from curious glances to friendly greetings. Zhoel waved to them, garnering smiles and shouts of encouragement. Even Tom gave him a polite nod as he and Simone passed, and Lila realized her cheeks hurt from smiling. God, she was having fun.

Zhoel attempted a turn, wobbled slightly, then adjusted, his balance steadying as he grasped the concept of moving backward with amazing quickness. He began switching from backward to forward with ease, then he coiled himself and surged forward, eating up the ice in long, powerful strides. His innate grace and power made her pulse quicken as she watched him round the rink, and she noticed more than a few female gazes openly admiring him as he passed. Even though their date wasn't real, Lila was suddenly filled with a sense of possessive pride.

He slowed to match her pace as he once again reached her side, and she linked her arm with his, thrilling at the sudden warmth of his body in the icy air. "I'm glad you're having fun."

He squeezed her arm more firmly against his side, looking down at her and smiling. "You are most pleasant company."

Her heart skipped a beat at the sincerity in his words. Suddenly self-conscious, she looked away. On the other side of the rink, she spotted Sara's son, Josh, struggling to stay upright on his skates. His arms flailed, his skates slipping unsteadily against the ice. On the bank several yards away, Sara was helping Emily make a snowman.

"Look, Aunt Lila!" Josh called out in a tremulous voice as Lila approached. "I'm skating!"

"Awesome job!" Lila encouraged, slowing.

Josh wobbled, skates scrabbling frantically, then crashed to the ground. He lay there, staring upward.

Lila hurried over to check on him. He blinked, looking more shocked than hurt. She held out a hand. "Oopsie! Let's try again."

Mouth turning down into a frown, Josh let out a repressed wail. He sat up, tears tracking down his chubby, chill-reddened cheeks.

"C'mon, Josh. You're okay," Lila encouraged. "Let's get up and try again."

Josh shook his head and shoved away her hand, his crying growing louder.

Zhoel had been watching in silence nearby. Suddenly, he windmilled his arms and crashed to the ice next to Josh. "Ouch!"

Josh's wailing hiccupped to a stop. He stared at Zhoel.

Lila was about to offer him help, but Zhoel made an exaggerated attempt to stand, thumping to the ice once more. "This is my first time skating," he admitted softly to Josh. "I don't know how to get up. Can you show me?"

Lila held back a smile, realizing what he was doing.

Josh wiped his nose on the back of his mitten and nodded. He rolled onto all fours and pushed himself up unsteadily. His movements were clumsy and ungraceful, but there was pride in his eyes as he finally stood straight.

Zhoel observed Josh carefully, mimicking his actions, including the scrabbling skates. "Like this?"

Lila fought back laughter at the sight of Zhoel's muscular backside poked high in the air.

He straightened, wobbled once, then beamed at Josh. "I did it! Thank you!"

Josh nodded, eyes now bright with the pride of teaching someone else. "Come on, Zhoel!" He clumped forward with short, stilted strides. "Let's race!"

Zhoel glanced at Lila, winked, and followed the boy, matching his slower pace.

Lila watched them go, her heart swelling with warmth as she headed toward Emily and Sara. The snowman they were building was a bit lopsided, with two unevenly placed rocks for eyes and a ragged scarf draped around its neck. Emily was patting more snow onto the snowman's lumpy base.

"How cute," Lila said with a smile as she approached them.

Sara kept wary eyes on Zhoel and Josh, who had reached the other side of the pond. "I have to admit, your alien's pretty good with kids."

"Zhoel's full of surprises," Lila said, putting an emphasis on his name. "Thank you for giving him the benefit of the doubt."

Sara made a noncommittal sound, watching the pair turn back toward them. Josh wobbled, arms flailing, but Zhoel deftly blocked his fall, helping him regain his balance. Confidence boosted, Josh lowered his head and powered forward, eyes glittering with excitement.

Zhoel followed close behind, his gaze on Lila strong as a physical touch. A little shudder of pleasure rolled through her.

Josh slid to a stop in front of his mother, breathing hard as he looked over his shoulder. "I beat you!" He grinned at Zhoel, who skidded to a stop beside him. "Mom, did you see?"

Sara nodded, gratitude shining in her eyes as she looked at Zhoel. "That was awesome!"

"He is an excellent teacher," said Zhoel.

"Let's do it again!" Josh said.

"How about we let Aunt Lila have her date back while we get some hot chocolate?" said Sara.

"Wanna come, Zhoel?" Josh asked.

Zhoel smiled and patted his head. "Not this time, thanks."

"Okay. See you later!"

They waved goodbye, and Lila leaned close. "You impressed Sara just now. Good job."

"That was not my goal, but I'm glad." He quirked an eyebrow and took her hand. "You obviously care for the boy, so I wanted to help."

Lila's heart skipped a beat. This fake date was feeling all too real. She could easily imagine spending more time with Zhoel, dancing, watching movies, talking late into the night. Being around Zhoel felt different from anything she'd known. But then again, hadn't she thought that once before? The memories of her relationship with Craig, its slow unraveling, lingered in the back of her mind. Zhoel's life was out there among the stars. He would eventually leave, just like Craig. And she'd be left behind to her responsibilities once again. No. She wouldn't let herself get attached.

She stared straight ahead at the ice as they skated, his grip on her hand making the butterflies in her stomach beat against her ribs. *This is simply physical attraction.* That was all she could let it be. But it'd been a long time since she'd been with a man, and her body was simply responding to his nearness and touch. Perhaps she needed to get it out of her system. It would be exciting to have some no-strings-attached fun.

As if in response to her thoughts, the familiar melody of *All I Want for Christmas is You* began to play. Zhoel turned and skated backward, taking her other hand. "Would you like to try a dance on the ice?"

"Sure," she said, trying to keep her voice steady.

She imagined the dance would be little more than holding hands while they took a turn around the pond, but Zhoel took the lead, pulling her close. Strides matching the rhythm of the music, he rotated them with liquid grace, hands firm against her waist. She leaned into him, feeling almost surreal as the twinkling lights and the distant laughter of children became nothing more than a soft backdrop to their own private dance.

Looking deep into her eyes, Zhoel guided her through a spin, their bodies separating, then reuniting gently as she came around, breasts pressed tightly against his chest. Her nipples ached, and every inch of her thrummed with desire. His warmth penetrated through their layers of clothing, his muscular thighs flexing against her. She slowly noticed something else pressing against her. Something undeniably hard. Her breath caught, a shiver tickling down her spine. *He's aroused, too.*

The music changed to *Have Yourself a Merry Little Christmas,* and Zhoel slowed their pace, warm breath caressing her cheek. His masculine scent left her panting from more than exertion. Their faces were inches apart, his hard length undeniable against her belly. There was a question in his eyes, yet he made no move to kiss her. Just like on the Ferris wheel. Was he waiting on her?

Insides trembling, Lila tugged at the front of his jacket, pulling his face down toward hers.

His lips met hers tentatively, as if he was testing the waters. But Lila didn't want tentative. Caught in a whirlwind of emotions and longing she hadn't allowed herself to feel for too long, she opened to him, flicking her tongue along the seam of his lips.

He responded with a soft groan, arms tightening around her and mouth claiming hers with unexpected and thrilling passion. One hand moved up her back to cup the back of her head, his thumb caressing the tender flesh below her ear.

She let go of his jacket and roved her hands up his broad chest, tracing the hard lines of his physique, hidden beneath layers of clothing. God, he was ripped. Warmth tingled between her legs and her breath grew ragged.

"Geez, get a room, you two." A voice startled her back to reality, and she pulled back, a rush of cool air flowing between them. A group of giggling teenagers stared in their direction as they skated past.

Zhoel straightened, brushing an errant lock of hair from Lila's flushed face, his hand lingering on her cheek for a moment. His eyes held a heat that rivaled the blazing fire pit. "That was… nice."

"We should…" Lila began, her voice a shaky whisper in the cold air. "We could continue this." Her attention darted to Zhoel's lips, then back to his eyes. "At my house."

Zhoel's gaze felt like it might burn the clothes right off her body. "I would like that very much, Lila."

7

Zhoel's heart thudded in anticipation as he and Lila strolled toward her family's house, her hand in his. Each breath clouded in the cold, but he barely felt the chill. All his senses were tuned to her presence. *Holding hands.* Who knew the simple gesture could be so thrilling?

He glanced at her again, taking in the way her dark hair fell around her face, each lock catching the soft light from the streetlamps above as they chatted. Her eyes were bright, and he could still feel the ghost of her lips on his, the warmth of her body pressed against his own. That kiss… it was more than just a meeting of lips. It was a connection, a spark that had ignited something deep within him.

*She is my mate.*

His Iki'i thrummed at the thought, and suddenly he knew it without a doubt. Zhoel had always assumed he wouldn't recognize his mate when he found her because of his flawed Iki'i, but the pull he felt toward Lila was like gravity drawing him in—undeniable. And based on her desire to continue their kiss in private, she seemed to feel the same way.

She was his mate. There could be no other explanation.

Ahead, Lila's house came into view, Christmas lights bright in each window. Zhoel's heart beat even faster. He imagined them slipping inside and finding a quiet corner where he could kiss her again, where he could hold her close and tell her everything that was in his heart.

Suddenly, Lila halted, her grip tightening around his hand. "Oh, no."

"What is it?" He looked at her in alarm.

"I forgot tonight is the family's annual white elephant exchange. Everyone's at the house." She pointed toward several cars parked in the driveway, their silhouettes dark against the snow.

Zhoel blinked, his universal translator filling his mind with an image of a lumbering, large-eared creature with an extended snout. "You exchange elephants for Christmas?"

Lila laughed. "No, not real elephants. It's the name of a game. Everyone brings a wrapped gift, and we take turns choosing or stealing them from each other."

"Stealing gifts?" Now he was even more baffled. "What does this have to do with elephants?"

"Uh, I don't know. But it's fun," she said, her smile widening. "Want to come? I have an extra gift you can bring."

He nodded. It wasn't the private moment he'd been hoping for, but it was an invitation to share in something that mattered to her and another human experience he could add to his list. "That sounds fascinating."

As she led him up the driveway, his HGU buzzed with an incoming message. He reached into his pocket and dismissed it without looking. It had buzzed him during their kiss, as well, but whatever it was could wait. He wanted to stay present in these moments.

Lila opened the front door, and they entered the house, enveloped in the sweet scent of hot cocoa and cookies. Chatter and laughter echoed from the living room, and Zhoel shrugged out of his coat, feeling Lila's shoulder brush against his as she hung her coat on a hook. The contact, though fleeting, sent a pleasant shiver over him. He caught her eye and found her watching him, a small, private smile playing at her lips. He returned it, astonished how a mere look from her could leave him feeling breathless.

Lila's mom poked her head around the corner. "Lila, you're here. Good." Her gaze slid to him, expression becoming guarded. "Is your friend joining us?"

"Yes, he is," Lila said with a hint of defiance in her tone. "I have an extra gift upstairs. Zhoel, please make yourself at home while I grab it." She gave his hand a quick squeeze, then darted toward the stairs.

Diane's lips pressed into a thin line, but she gestured for Zhoel to follow her. "Come on. Everyone's in the living room."

Zhoel suddenly felt very conspicuous without Lila by his side. The scene in the living room only heightened his unease. At least twenty people sat around the space, far more than had attended dinner last night, and the noise was a dull roar in his ears—laughter, conversations, the excited shouts of children. The overall mood was eager excitement, but there were so many people, he had to repress his Iki'i to avoid a headache.

"Zhoel!" Josh bounded from amongst the crowd, skidding to a stop in front of him. "You're here!" The child grabbed his hand. "Come on! You have to see the presents!"

Zhoel let himself be pulled forward, unable to resist the boy's enthusiasm. People stared as he passed, but many of them smiled, and his tension lightened. The lights on the tree twinkled brightly, casting a festive glow over the gathering. Brightly wrapped gifts had been placed beneath the low boughs, and several other children stood near it, practically vibrating with anticipation.

"These ones are for kids." Josh pointed to a pile that was set a little apart from the others, his face scrunched up in contemplation. "Which one do you think has the best toy?"

Zhoel wasn't sure what constituted a good gift in this human game, but he tried to play along, pointing to a long one wrapped in red striped paper with a large white bow on top. "I think that one looks interesting."

Someone nudged his elbow, and he turned to see Aunt Maggie at his side. His throat tightened, worried about what she might say. "Hello Maggie."

She winked at him. "I'd stay away from gifts that look too perfect. Those always turn out to be lemons."

He frowned. First elephants, now lemons? "Lemons are bad?"

Maggie chortled and nudged him again. "Well, I suppose they might make you pucker up." She pursed her lips and batted her eyes coyly. "Though I hear you and Lila have already been doing that."

Zhoel's cheeks warmed. Before Aunt Maggie could continue, he caught sight of Nana Pearl waving at him from across the room. Relief washed over him like a cool breeze, and he offered Aunt Maggie a polite nod. "If you'll excuse me, I think Nana Pearl is trying to get my attention."

Maggie's eyes twinkled with amusement, but she

stepped back, allowing him to move away. "Of course."

Zhoel pressed through the crowd toward the elderly matriarch. She sat in an armchair with a ball of yarn in her lap and two long, pointed sticks gripped in her gnarled fingers. "I was hoping I'd get a chance to speak with you," she said, smiling and setting aside the sticks. "How has your date with Lila been? It's been a while since I've seen her this happy."

A pang of guilt twisted in Zhoel's chest at the reminder of the misunderstanding Nana Pearl had over his email. Not that it mattered now. What had begun as a business trip had become something with far more important ramifications for his future; thanks to Nana, he'd found his mate. He smiled at her. "It's been a long time since I've been this happy, too."

Something soft brushed against his leg and he glanced down to see the fluffy orange family pet weaving around his ankles. He bent and stroked its head.

"Oh, my. I'm surprised the cat lets you pet him," said Nana. "He hates everyone except Adam."

*Cat.* Zhoel catalogued the name for his translator. "He was in my room last night."

"Sorry about that," called Lila's dad from his chair. "But if you can make Whiskers like you, you're okay in my book."

Zhoel grinned. Good thing he'd realized the creature was a pet last night instead of assuming it was vermin.

One of the children squealed, sending the cat darting off to hide under a nearby chair. Zhoel straightened and spotted Lila making her way toward the tree with a pair of wrapped gifts in her arms. Their eyes met, and she smiled, the sight sending a familiar thrill through him.

"Looks like we're about to get started," Nana Pearl said, following his gaze. "Better get back to your date."

The air buzzed with playful energy as people found their spots, some sitting cross-legged on the floor, others perched on the edge of chairs. Zhoel joined Lila standing at one end of a long sofa. The soft glow of the Christmas lights reflected in her eyes, her smile radiating pure joy as she looked around at her family.

The rules of the game were explained quickly for the children, then they went first, laughing and trading rather than stealing. It seemed none of the gifts were undesirable, and the children scampered away, happy to play while the adults continued the game.

As numbers were handed out for the order of choosing gifts, Lila leaned close and whispered, "Don't overthink it. Just pick whichever gift catches your eye. The fun part is the trading… or trying to avoid trading."

He nodded, aware of every point where their bodies touched, of the subtle scent of her hair—like vanilla and something floral. It took a conscious effort to focus on the game and not just on her.

The first few rounds went by in a blur of laughter and light-hearted banter. Gifts were unwrapped to reveal things like a snowman-shaped mug or a pair of fuzzy socks. Lila took a turn and got a box of something she called hot cocoa mix. "We can drink it later," she told him as more presents were swapped and stolen, the lively energy growing with each turn. It was a dance of sorts, a series of strategic moves and light-hearted thefts that brought out the playful side in everyone.

Tom's turn arrived, and he scanned the pile of gifts thoughtfully before picking a huge, brightly wrapped box. He unwrapped it with a flourish, revealing another festive box inside. The room erupted in laughter as he opened boxes of decreasing size. Finally, he groaned dramatically. "Dog gone it. Not the snow globe!" His gaze zeroed in on Lila. He strode over and swapped the snow globe for her hot chocolate. "Yoink!"

"Tom!" Lila cried in mock outrage as everyone laughed. "You'd steal from your own sister?"

Zhoel leaned close, eyes fixed on the bauble. It depicted a scene of dancing elves, a sleigh with a wildly waving Santa, and penguins skating on an ice rink. "I thought your family valued these items," he said.

Lila laughed and wound a key on the bottom. The ornament emitted a scratchy tune he didn't recognize, but that sounded cringingly off key. "This is the first snow globe from our family's collection," Lila said. "Grandpa brought it back when my dad was just a boy, and it's been re-gifted ever since. It makes it feel like he's still a part of the gift exchange every year."

He smiled, appreciating how her family valued keeping past loved ones present.

Tom's girlfriend Simone went next, receiving a neon green throw blanket she swapped for Tom's hot chocolate. She leaned in to give him a quick kiss on the cheek. "All's fair in love and gift exchanges."

Tom laughed. "How 'bout we share our gifts later?"

Zhoel glanced at Lila, thinking something similar, and caught her watching him. With a smile, she turned back to the gift exchange, laying her cheek against his arm. Joy spread through him like a warm beverage on a chilly day. He wanted to feel this way forever.

When it was Zhoel's turn, he moved forward to examine the remaining gifts. He chose a flat box that felt light in his hands, opening it slowly. Inside, he found a plain green sweater, various colorful felt pieces, pom-poms, miniature bells, and a tube of glue. "What is this?"

"It's a kit to make an ugly Christmas sweater," Lila explained, her grin widening at his confusion. "You going to keep it or swap it?"

He licked his lips, uncertain he was ready to steal gifts from her family, even in play. "Why would anyone want to create an ugly garment intentionally?"

"I don't know. It's a tradition." Lila shrugged.

"It's from the Depression," Nana called across the room, lifting her needles to drape a long swath of cloth down toward her lap. "From when people needed sweaters for warmth rather than style."

"Nana, we love your sweaters," Lila said, joined by agreeing nods and shouts from the rest of the family.

Zhoel looked down at the kit again. "Then I shall keep this gift."

Lila laughed, looping her arm through his. "I'll help you decorate it later."

When the last gift had been claimed, the family dispersed, a few leaving for home, some heading toward the kitchen for more snacks, others chatting in small groups. Lila led Zhoel to the den. "We can have a little privacy in here until everyone goes home. Let's put your sweater together while we wait."

The promise in her eyes made his groin ache with need, but he kept himself in check as they moved to the den. Lila turned on the fireplace and pulled over a low table. She took his sweater kit and began spreading the contents across the table in a chaotic array of colors and textures. "Let's see what kind of masterpiece we can make."

They settled on the rug, shoulders brushing, and Lila explained how to attach the felt pieces to the sweater. Zhoel watched her closely, more focused on the way her lips moved, the way her hair fell around her face, than on her instructions. They were so close, just a breath apart, and he could feel her heartbeat echoing his own, fast and unsteady.

She looked up, and he realized she'd asked him a question. But the moment their gazes connected, the air between them seemed to thicken. Without thinking, he leaned in, his lips brushing hers.

She responded immediately, her hands sliding up his chest and around his neck. The kiss deepened, became more urgent, a spark igniting into heat that spread through him like magma. His need was both thrilling and terrifying in its intensity. He wrapped an arm around her waist, pulling her tightly against him, her breasts soft against his chest.

"I never imagined I'd actually find my mate," he murmured against her lips.

Lila's breath hitched. "Mate?" She pulled back, the word hanging between them like an icicle about to drop. "We're just kissing."

He felt his chest tighten with familiar anxiety. He'd misread situations too many times in the past, letting his emotions cloud his judgment. Had this entire day been a mistake? Before he could say anything, the sudden, sharp rap of knuckles on the doorframe demanded attention.

Diane stood there, looking none too pleased. "Zhoel, there's someone at the door for you."

Confused, Zhoel followed Diane out, Lila close at his side. Who would be looking for him here?

In the foyer, a tall Kirenai in a white and yellow Intergalactic Dating Agency uniform stood waiting, his blue face stern. Zhoel's stomach filled with icy dread. *The messages I ignored.* He pulled his HGU from his pocket, but didn't have time to read it.

"I'm here on behalf of the permitting office," the IDA representative said, his tone formal and cold. "You are to cease all business here on Earth and return to the orbital station immediately."

Zhoel's fists clenched in frustration at his sides. *Kuzara.* The IDA must have caught wind of his plans. "What seems to be the problem?"

Lila's hand slipped into his, squeezing lightly. He held onto the sensation, needing it to steady himself. Her family had gathered to look in from the living room, their whispers a low, anxious hum.

"There's a problem with your visa. Please avoid making an intergalactic scene and return to the station with me now."

Before Zhoel could ask what the problem was, Nana Pearl stepped forward, her voice surprisingly firm. "He hasn't finished his date with my granddaughter yet. He'll come along when they're done."

Zhoel groaned inwardly. Nana Pearl didn't realize the gravity of her words—by galactic law, all romantic relationships with humans had to be coordinated by the IDA. It was one reason he was so determined to get his business up and running, to break their stranglehold over the market.

"I see," the representative said, raising his eyebrows and smirking slightly. "Then this is definitely a violation." He pulled out a pair of cuffs. "Zhoel Aedul, you're under arrest."

8

Lila gaped at the blue-skinned IDA representative standing amidst her family's scattered coats and boots in the foyer. He looked like he was made of plastic, with coifed hair and a perfectly creased white uniform. Two loops of metal in his hand shimmered with an odd, almost liquid quality—alien handcuffs, she assumed. "You're arresting him for dating me?" she asked, cheeks heating with anger. "That's ridiculous!"

Her parents and several other curious family members crowded nearby in the archway to the living room, exchanging whispers about what was happening.

The IDA representative smiled at her and looked down his nose. "Beautiful humans like you are in high demand across the galaxy, my dear, often abducted for nefarious purposes. We wouldn't want you to end up sold on the black market, now, would we?" He shifted his attention back to Zhoel and raised a blue eyebrow. "As Zhoel knows, the IDA is the only agency licensed to coordinate travel to Earth for romantic interactions."

That got Lila's hackles up. She'd had enough of Nana meddling in her love life, let alone an alien government. "I don't give a rip about your licensing," she said, looping her arm possessively around Zhoel's. "I'm perfectly capable of screening my own suitors, and Zhoel has been nothing but a gentleman, thank you very much."

Zhoel looked down at her, gratitude and something more in his eyes. He held out a small circular device, activating a hovering screen full of blue alien script. Lila's eyes widened at this glimpse of alien technology, and her family's murmuring intensified. Zhoel extended the device toward the rep. "As you can see, my visa permit has been fully approved. It is for business, but it doesn't specify what type of interactions I can have with humans while I'm here."

The rep held out the cuffs. "A technicality you'll need to take up with the permitting office." Lila's stomach tightened as their metallic sheen glinted under the hallway light. "Come with me now, and I'll see what I can do about keeping this infraction off your permanent record."

Aunt Maggie elbowed her way forward between Lila's parents. "Do you have a warrant? Exactly what is your jurisdiction?"

A flicker of uncertainty crossed the rep's blue features. "I'm here on behalf of the Confederation of Planets. Zhoel has violated his business visa, which is an intergalactic—"

"This is Earth," said Maggie, hands going to her hips. "To my knowledge, we have not yet been accepted into the Confederation of Planets. And we don't arrest people without proper paperwork or proof of wrongdoing."

The rep straightened, his jaw tightening. "I'm fully authorized to—"

"Show me a warrant or get out." Aunt Maggie's five-foot-five frame seemed to grow as she yanked her phone from her purse. "I work for a law firm, and I'll have a team of lawyers filing legal complaints against you personally if you proceed without proper Earth protocols. What is your name and authorization? I'll send it to them now."

The rep's scowl deepened, attention flicking to Zhoel, then back to Maggie before he jerked open the front door. "You've only delayed the inevitable, you know. I'll be back soon with your Earth arrest warrant."

The door slammed behind him in a puff of cold air, and Lila released a breath, legs feeling suddenly weak. She realized she was still clutching Zhoel's arm, let go, and grasped Aunt Maggie's hands. "That was amazing."

Zhoel bowed deeply. "You have my sincere gratitude, Aunt Maggie."

"Well, I couldn't see you two lovebirds separated just as you're starting to get your wings." Aunt Maggie's face crinkled back into her usual grin. "I'm just glad I didn't need to get Walter on the phone."

Lila grinned back, picturing Walter Higgins, Maggie's elderly boss and the only lawyer in Bloomington, arguing intergalactic law with aliens. "I would've liked to see that, actually."

Mom's voice sliced through the levity. "Will one of you please tell me what's going on? You two told me Zhoel was here for a date. What's this about a business visa?"

Guilt shot up Lila's spine and she struggled to find the right words. "Can't he be here for both business and a date?"

Mom's eyes flashed with fury. "You lied to me! We don't conduct business over the holidays for a reason, Lila. Everyone's emotions are already running high. Look at all the stress you caused. You're going to give your dad another heart attack."

"Diane, stop fretting." Dad put an arm around Mom's shoulders. "I'm fine. Let's go back to the living room and sit down."

Mom gave him a worried look. "Yes, you need to sit. Don't worry about any of this. I'll handle it."

Lila's jaw tensed, and frustration burned in her throat. "We have bills to pay, Mom. And our creditors don't give a crap if it's the holidays or not. We can't afford to miss out on this opportunity." She took a quick breath, smiled at her dad, and steadied her voice. "Listen. I don't want to stress anyone, but ignoring matters will cause more stress in the long run. The company needs to make some changes soon or we'll lose everything. Zhoel and I are working on a plan to secure a future for both our companies."

Tom poked his head over Dad's shoulder. "If Zhoel came here on business, why was he kissing you at the skating pond today?" His eyes narrowed on Zhoel. "This alien could be trying to manipulate you. I've heard they have empathic power to control people's emotions."

Lila opened her mouth to reply, but froze. She'd heard something about that, too. Was she so desperate to save the business, she was letting Zhoel cloud her judgment?

Zhoel stood still as a statue, blue skin darkening with what might be a flush. "I didn't come here to manipulate anyone," he said in a low monotone. "I came here to coordinate a partnership with a transportation supplier. Whatever feelings Lila and I have developed are separate from that."

Lila swallowed, Tom's accusation sinking deeper than she wanted to admit. It felt as if the ground was shifting beneath her as Zhoel's words in the den repeated themselves in her head. *I never imagined I'd actually find my mate.* Was he manipulating her? They'd barely known each other a single day. How could he possibly think she was his mate? Yet a part of her own mind insisted the connection was real, despite any attempt at rationality.

Mom moved past her and grabbed Zhoel's peacoat from the rack by the door, handing it to him. "I think it's best if you go get your visa figured out. You can contact us again after the holidays."

Panic surged in Lila's chest. If he left now, he might never come back. Regardless of any personal entanglements, she still believed Zhoel's plan could be the key to saving the family business. And this whole mate thing still needed to be unraveled. She snatched the coat from her mother's hand, glaring at her. "I live here, too, and Zhoel is my guest. You can't just throw him out because you're upset."

"Lila's right, Diane," said Dad. "Let's all just go to bed and we can deal with everything in the morning."

Mom pressed her lips into a thin line, but after several moments, released a pent-up breath that Lila was surprised didn't burst into flame. "Fine. But he leaves first thing in the morning. And I'd better not hear anyone creeping around the hallway in the middle of the night."

Heat filled Lila's face, and Zhoel shifted uncomfortably. Her earlier hopes of being alone with him felt ridiculous now.

Tom huffed, arms crossed over his chest. "You want me to stay in my old room tonight, Mom? Help keep an eye on things? I still have that old air rifle in the attic."

Zhoel stiffened and shot her a look of alarm.

"Oh, good Lord!" Lila threw her hands into the air. "We're all adults. I don't need a babysitter."

"He's an alien, Lila. Who knows what he's capable of?" Tom insisted.

Lila poked her brother hard in the chest. "You don't know anything about him, you jerk. He's been nothing but respectful."

"I would never harm Lila or her family," Zhoel said.

Dad gave Zhoel an apologetic glance, then handed Tom his coat. "Everything here will be fine, Tom. You take Simone home. We'll see you tomorrow."

"Adam—" Mom started, her voice tight.

Dad held up a hand. "I've been on the road without a bed too many times, Diane. We won't do that to anyone, much less someone who we've already invited to stay. Lila, why don't you take Zhoel to the guest room? We'll see everybody off."

Zhoel pressed his palms together and bowed his head toward her father. "I am grateful for your hospitality."

Relief washed over Lila, but her heart still beat too fast. She quickly led Zhoel up the stairs, the sounds of her family murmuring and shuffling into their coats drifting up the stairwell. Tension vibrated like electricity in the silence between her and Zhoel. Despite everything that had happened, she felt all fluttery inside. *I want to kiss him again.*

At the door to the guest room, he turned to her, eyes filled with distress. "Our plan to impress your family isn't going very well."

The flutter in her chest turned to something heavier: doubt. *Our plan.* Had he only kissed her because of a business scheme? No, it couldn't be. In the den, he'd suggested she was his mate. But what if that had been for show, too? Part of the fake date in case her family was eavesdropping. *What if Tom's right?* What if what she felt wasn't real? The sudden and intense attraction differed from anything she'd ever experienced. It couldn't be normal.

"Have you been manipulating my emotions?" she blurted.

Zhoel's skin darkened to midnight blue. "Absolutely not," he said, his tone firm, but something flickered in his gaze. Something he was hiding.

"But your species can manipulate emotions, right?"

He hugged his arms across his chest and frowned. "Not exactly. Kirenai can read emotions and use that for more favorable interactions." He took her hands. "But Lila, I would never manipulate you. I can't."

Her stomach churned with uncertainty. "Well, we can stop the fake dating now. My family knows everything."

Zhoel's expression tightened. "It's not fake, Lila. Something happened between us on the ice. A Kirenai knows when he's found his mate, and I've found mine."

*There he goes again, using that word; mate.* As if she were the one woman destined to be with him for all eternity. The idea seemed like a fairytale. One that she wanted to believe all too much. But could she trust anything he said right now, much less this? She pulled her hands from his. "I'm not sure about this whole mate thing. Let's keep our focus on business for now." She turned toward her room, choking out at the last minute, "Goodnight."

He called softly after her, "Goodnight, Lila."

She closed her bedroom door behind her and locked it—not that she worried about Zhoel, but as a reminder to herself to stay put. That kiss on the ice had seared itself into her memory like a brand on her soul. Even the thought of his lips against hers sent a tingle of heat between her legs.

Her attraction was quickly becoming an obsession, and it frightened her. Zhoel was hiding something, she was certain. Undressing, she eased between the sheets, trying to numb her spinning thoughts. But no matter her doubts, her mind still kept circling back to that kiss. His hands in hers as they glided around the ice, their bodies pressed together. On instinct, her fingers crept down her belly, sliding into the front of her panties.

She let out a small gasp of pleasure as her middle finger slid over her swollen clit. She pressed the sensitive nub, hoping to ease the throbbing, but it only made her need more. *Maybe I simply need a release.*

Dipping deeper between her folds, she pulled the slickness up and over, circling while picturing Zhoel's naked blue chest above her. She imagined his hands pressing her thighs apart, gaze hot on her center.

The panties were hampering her movement, so she kicked out of them, then let one hand trail up her stomach under her shirt, cupping a breast through the thin fabric of her bra. Pinching a hardened nipple, she imagined it was Zhoel's mouth suckling and nipping.

As she rubbed her clit, she imagined Zhoel's imaginary cock thrusting into her again and again, until she convulsed with the shock of release. She lay there gasping, yet incomplete.

*I still want him.* She pulled the covers over her bare legs and stared up at the ceiling. Such an intense and persistent lust had to be alien manipulation, right?

*No.* When it came down to it, Lila trusted Zhoel. He was respectful, funny, good with kids, and an excellent kisser. Although he'd come to dinner under false pretenses, he'd told her the truth the first chance he got. And she couldn't blame him for accepting Nana's invitation: Nana Pearl could be as much of a bulldozer as Mom when she wanted to. Zhoel was telling the truth when he said he believed they were mates.

Rolling onto her side, she drew the covers over her head, listening to the quiet of the sleeping house. She didn't doubt Zhoel's intentions, but perhaps she should question her own. Did she truly believe they could be mates as he continued to insist? Or was she letting herself fall for him because he was a way to save her family's company?

9

Zhoel stood in the dark, staring at the flicker of Christmas lights on the snow outside his window. Their cheerful glow felt distant, like a life he could never touch. Although he respected Lila's decision to keep their focus on business for now, her emotional withdrawal stung. The attraction he'd felt growing between them had been replaced by the cold emptiness of distrust. He couldn't blame her—not after he'd failed to tell her the truth about his faulty Iki'i.

*Maybe she's right to doubt me.* What if their connection wasn't real? After all, he'd misinterpreted his Iki'i time and again.

No. That couldn't be right—every part of him felt the truth of it, coursing through his body like a low, thrumming pulse. His Iki'i had never been this insistent before. This tangible. When she was near, the connection between them didn't waver. The more he thought about it, the more his chest tightened. *Her nearness makes me stronger.* Kirenai didn't bond without reason. He felt Lila was his as sure as his own heartbeat, and delaying that truth until morning would only let her doubts eat away at whatever trust she had left.

He moved to the door and peered into the dark, silent hallway, heart pounding with a mix of trepidation and determination. The house was silent, the hallway lit only by the ambient glow of Christmas lights from downstairs. He'd agreed to her mother's request not to move around the house during the night out of respect, but every moment that passed allowed more room for Lila to slip further away. And with his visa situation, he might not have much time left.

He needed to tell her about his flaw, and he needed to tell her now. It was the only way they could move forward, the only way she could truly understand his feelings for her. He knew the risks—she might reject him, might think him weak or incapable. But he also knew that the connection between them was real, and he couldn't let it slip away because of fear.

Moving quietly, he stepped into the hallway toward Lila's door. As he reached to knock, a wave of aroused desire nearly bowled him over. He hesitated, body instantly heating in response. *Could this be from Lila?* Though his Iki'i felt stronger around her, he still didn't trust his interpretation. For all he knew, she could be inside sobbing with grief.

He took a deep breath and knocked softly on her door.

The sound of startled movement came from somewhere inside. After another few heartbeats, Lila opened the door, looking flushed and breathless. She wore a short nightshirt that clung to her curves and exposed her long, well-toned legs. An unmistakable drift of pheromones filled his senses, and he groaned involuntarily. *Kuzara,* she was magnificent.

"Zhoel?" she breathed, her voice barely above a whisper. She grabbed his arm and pulled him inside, shutting the door behind him. "Come in before someone sees you."

He entered, barely able to take in the room as dizzying waves of lust buffeted his senses. Before he could stop himself, he reached for her. Though instinct drove him forward, his logic braced for a rebuke. *What am I doing?* She'd been quite clear about her wish to keep their relationship professional.

His heart soared as she yielded eagerly to his embrace, rising to her toes and pressing her lips to his. *My Lila.*

He wrapped his arms around her, pulling her closer, deepening the kiss. Her hands roamed up his back, rucking his shirt up to skim her palms over his skin. The feather-light touch fanned the flames of his longing, making his mating rod stiffen to aching hardness.

He drew back just enough to whisper against her lips, "This isn't what I came here for."

"I don't care. I can't stop thinking about you." She gripped the hem of his shirt and pulled it over his head, pressing hot, wet kisses over his chest.

Groaning, Zhoel trailed a hand down the curve of her spine, pulling her hips against his. He cupped her ass, her flesh hot through the thin fabric of her nightshirt. Putting one hand beneath her jaw, he guided her back into a kiss, plunging his tongue into her again and again until she drew one leg up and wrapped it around his hip, her center exposed and hot. *She isn't wearing panties.* Another moan escaped his lips. This woman would undo him.

His cock throbbed with anticipation and he gripped the smooth roundness of her ass, fingertips brushing the heated folds of her sex. She gasped, arching her back as he glided across her soaked cleft. He pressed between the folds, teasing the soft flesh as she rocked her hips against him and emitted small whimpers of pleasure.

As he trailed a line of kisses down her neck, his Iki'i thrummed with the pleasure of her arousal. This was how it felt to be complete. To have a mate who could share the joys of the universe with him.

Finding the swollen nodule of her clit, he circled it and murmured, "Tell me you feel the connection between us."

"God, Zhoel," she gasped. "I don't want to talk right now. Please, just fuck me."

His desire for her was nearly overpowering, but her words made him pause. He'd misread his Iki'i yet again. She wanted him, but didn't really believe she was his mate.

*You can't force such a thing.* The choice had to be hers. But he could at least enjoy her pleasure tonight.

"As you wish." Grasping her under the ass with both hands, he carried her to the bed.

Lila's every fantasy about Zhoel paled in the reality of his touch. Her body was on fire, every nerve ending alight with desire. She could barely think straight. Sex had never been this intense with Craig—or anyone else, for that matter. And she knew one thing for certain: she felt something more between her and Zhoel, something powerful. Her brain wanted to deny it, but the rest of her body seemed to think otherwise.

Zhoel lowered her onto the mattress and stood there a moment, looking down at her with eyes dark as midnight. He growled low in his throat, sending shivers down her spine before reaching out and tearing her nightgown down the front. Holy hell, she'd always dreamed of having a man rip her clothes off. His gaze lingered over her breasts like a caress, then settled on her pussy. He looked like a predator preparing to consume his prey, and a gush of moisture coated her thighs.

Never taking his gaze from her sex, he reached for his fly, flicking it open to expose a thick blue shaft with rows of nodules along its length. Her breath caught. Alien peen looked a lot like her vibrator.

His pants slid down his hips, and he stepped free, pushing a knee between her legs to part her thighs. Planting a hand to either side of her hips, he lowered his head and rubbed a rough cheek up the inside of her soft flesh until his breath fanned hotly across her sex.

She flexed her hips, yearning for his touch, but he only inhaled deeply before moving to the other thigh. This time he skimmed his lips over her skin, tongue flicking out to leave cooling trails of moisture along the way. He stopped just shy of her pussy, sucking and licking ever so slowly toward her center.

Lila squirmed, fingers tangled in his hair as she urged him on. It was as if he knew exactly what she needed, exactly how to touch her to elicit the most intense pleasure. She could feel his desire, his need for her, as acutely as her own. It was overwhelming, all-consuming, and she never wanted it to end.

His mouth reached her pussy, licking, sucking, probing. His tongue swept along her cleft, circling her clit until she thought she'd come undone, but he stopped just short of giving her release.

"Zhoel, please," she begged, clamping her thighs against his cheeks.

He chuckled, and his hands pressed her legs apart, lifting her knees so he could delve deeper. His tongue penetrated her, deeper and fuller than any human tongue ought to be, while a thumb circled her clit. He stretched and filled her until she cried out, bucking up to take it, shudders of pleasure coursing through her body. And yet, as the wave subsided, it wasn't enough. She wanted all of him.

Grabbing his hair, she tugged him toward her. "Come to me now, Zhoel."

Prowling up her body, he paused only to suck each nipple in turn before claiming her mouth with his. He pressed his hips to hers, the bumps on his shaft sliding over her clit. He pumped a few times, rubbing her swollen nub until she wrapped her legs around him, flexing up with unspoken need. Pulling back, he entered her in one slick thrust, sending exquisite pleasure through her.

She cried out, and he paused, breath heaving and body trembling as he let her adjust to his girth. "Don't stop," she whimpered.

He cupped her face, looking down into her eyes as he began to pump in and out, slowly picking up speed. She wasn't sure which was more intense, his gaze or his purposeful strokes. Under her fingers, the muscles of his back rippled and flexed as he thrust until her eyes fluttered closed, heart feeling like it was going to burst.

He slammed home again and again, mouth on hers, one hand gripping the back of her neck. Leaning close to her ear, he growled, "You're mine, Lila."

His words made her orgasm hit her like a freight train. Her back arched, her body convulsed, her inner muscles clamping down as waves of pleasure washed over her. She cried out his name, her voice muffled by his kisses as he rode her through the ecstasy. As her spasms subsided, Zhoel shuddered and groaned, his cock jerking inside her.

Lila gulped for air, unsure where her sweat-slicked skin ended and his began.

Finally, Zhoel lifted himself and rolled to one side. As his cock left her, warm fluid dribbled between her thighs and sudden alarm spiked in her chest. She turned to look at him. "We didn't use protection."

He stared up at the ceiling and shook his head. "There's no worry. I didn't claim you."

"Claim me?"

"My Icky'ee still insists you're my perfect mate," he said. "But if you don't feel it, too, I won't claim you."

She frowned. "Zhoel, we've only known each other a day. How can you possibly think I'm your... mate?"

He sighed and turned to look at her. "I know it seems sudden. But Kirenai connections aren't like human ones. When we find our mate, it hits us deep and fast. Our Iki'i knows. I can't explain it any better than that." He clenched his fists, as if resisting the urge to pull her against him. "I just... I never conceived of finding a mate. I have a... flaw. I lost my whole family because of it."

Shocked, Lila sat up. "They died?"

Zhoel took a deep breath and pulled the blanket up to cover them. "No, I'm being melodramatic. I should say estranged. Do you remember I mentioned my parents own a chain of luxury hotels?"

She nodded.

"My family... they had high expectations, especially my father. He tasked me with brokering a sale of a hotel in the Ariff nebula to the Volran Corporation. Their CEO was a fogarian woman—"

Lila's brows furrowed slightly. "Fogarian? What's that?"

"Humanoid, but with ochre skin and clawed fingers," he replied.

She thought she'd seen aliens like that on a documentary, so she encouraged him to continue. "What happened?"

"I've struggled with interpreting my empathic senses all my life, and thought I sensed cunning and desperation from the CEO. I didn't want to look like a pushover on my first deal, so I pressed harder than I should've. In reality, she was cautious and felt disrespected. She walked away from the deal, and worse, from all future dealings with our company." Zhoel's voice roughened. "We lost millions. My father was furious and said I was a disgrace to the family name. That I was too weak to be a Kirenai. He passed control of the company to my brother. I haven't spoken to any of them since."

Lila reached out and took his hand. "It sounds like he should've been furious with that CEO, not you." She thought of her own mother and scowled. "God, why do parents have to be so critical?"

Zhoel shrugged. "I've learned to be okay. I left home to travel, and that led me to you. I know you don't feel the same way I do, but I'm grateful to have found you."

She searched his eyes for any ounce of doubt, but found none. *He really believes I'm his mate.* And she couldn't deny the strong connection she felt with him, both physical and emotional. Hardly able to believe what she was about to say, she squeezed his hand. "I'm not saying I'm your mate, but... I think our connection is real."

A smile like a sunbeam spread across Zhoel's face, and he cupped her cheek, stroking his thumb across her lips. "Maybe we should try to verify it again."

## 10

Sunlight streamed through a gap in the bedroom curtains, warming the tangled sheets as Zhoel watched Lila sleep in his arms. He couldn't stop marveling at the curve of her cheek, the way her dark lashes rested against her skin. He'd spent the last few hours learning the contours of her body, exulting in the way his Iki'i spiked with pleasure whenever her breath hitched at his touch. Each time he'd carried her over the brink, he'd fought to restrain himself from using his secondary mating rod and sealing the bond. She said she'd think about becoming his mate, but until she agreed, he would simply let her savor the slow burn of their connection.

Lila sighed and stretched against him, her chestnut hair spilling across the pillow. He watched her eyelids flutter open, hazel eyes blinking sleepily in the morning light. She smiled and glided one palm over his bare chest with a familiarity that made his heart soar.

"Morning," she murmured, her voice husky with sleep.

"Good morning." Zhoel pressed a languid kiss to her temple, inhaling her warm sweet scent. At once, his cock rose to full attention, rock hard against her hip.

Lila flexed against it, a pleased glint in her eye. "Are you always this ready to go?"

"For you, yes." His voice was rough, every blood vessel in his body thrumming with need. *Kuzara*, she had no idea.

Her hand slid down his belly toward his shaft, but the patter of small running feet in the hallway outside made her freeze. She sighed, then slowly pulled away and sat up. "We should probably get dressed before someone starts knocking on doors."

Zhoel nodded, reluctantly sliding out of the warm sheets to pick up his pants. As he pulled them on, his

HGU vibrated in his pocket. A knot of dread tightened his gut. He'd become so caught up in the moment with Lila that he'd forgotten all about the IDA and his potential arrest.

Pulling the device from his pocket, he brought up the hologram and saw the message he'd been dreading. "Kuzara," he groaned.

Lila pulled a heavy sweater over her head and stepped into a pair of jeans before moving closer to peer at the device. "What's it say?"

He scanned the contents of several missed messages, his stomach churning at the escalation of warnings. "The permitting office is saying I violated the terms of my travel. If I don't resolve things in the next few hours, they'll arrest me."

He activated the connection to the interplanetary permitting office. After a few moments, a hologram of a tall, alabaster-skinned vatosangan with large, hooded purple eyes and a pinched nose appeared. "Interplanetary Permitting, Earth Division."

Zhoel cleared his throat, quickly assessing the man's black uniform tunic. No IDA insignia, at least not visibly, but he knew many of the permitting officials received kickbacks from the IDA. Choosing his words carefully, he said, "I received a notice about an issue with my visa."

"Name and visa ID," the official said in a disinterested voice.

Zhoel rattled off the information. The pause that followed stretched uncomfortably, the vatosangan's thin indigo lips becoming thinner as he reviewed the information until each beat of Zhoel's heart felt like the ticking of a bomb.

Lila's fingers laced with his and squeezed gently, reminding him to breathe. He smiled gratefully at her, unused to having someone supporting him. He'd always pursued his goals alone, and that made the weight of his mistakes heavier. But now, with Lila beside him, his burdens didn't feel so crushing.

Finally, the official's indigo eyebrows drew into a single confused line. "It appears there was a problem with your arrival coordinates. There's something here about... cultural interference?"

Zhoel's chest tightened as he recalled his arrival among the religious statuary. Surely, they couldn't reprimand him for that mistake? He gritted his teeth. The IDA was obviously attempting to twist the situation to their advantage. They'd do anything to undermine potential competition. "I used the human database to plot my coordinates and teleported to Bloomington, just as approved on my application. Did the human authorities submit a complaint?"

"The complaint was filed anonymously."

Scowling, Lila put a hand on his wrist and turned the hologram to face her. "People were just surprised to see him, but there's no issue with him being here. I live here, and I'll vouch for him."

The official blinked, hooded gaze widening with interest at seeing Lila. Zhoel tensed at the official's obvious appreciation, but schooled his features to remain calm; showing animosity wouldn't help his cause.

The official cleared his throat. "Yes, well, you can testify during the audit. Until then, Zhoel Aedul is being ordered to leave the surface and remain outside orbital limits until the matter is resolved."

Zhoel clenched his fists, trying to suppress his rising panic. He knew how this would play out. Once he left Earth, the IDA would tie him up in bureaucracy, ensuring he'd never be able to return to finish his business or see Lila again.

Praying this official wasn't on the IDA's payroll, he leaned forward and dropped his voice. "Listen. I'm developing an app—an intergalactic dating and travel platform to open rural communities like Bloomington to alien visitors. The IDA doesn't want the competition, and they're using this audit to push me out. I need your help."

The official blinked, his gaze returning to Zhoel with sudden interest. "A travel app? I thought the IDA had the exclusive contract for Earth."

"They do, but they focus exclusively on creating matches, not experiencing Earth culture. I want to focus on more than dating. I want to provide quality interactions that help the galaxy understand humans and their traditions. But I can't do that if the IDA forces me to leave. Is there any way you can help me?" Zhoel held his breath.

There was a beat of silence, then the official shifted in his seat, his voice a low, conspiratorial whisper. "How, exactly, would one sign up for your app?"

Exhaling with hopeful relief, Zhoel said, "It's still in development, but if you give me your contact information, I can add you to our beta testing list."

The official glanced over his shoulder as though ensuring no one else was watching. "Considering the cultural significance of your work," he said, tapping something on his console, "I can reclassify your visa under scientific study, providing broader travel clearance. This should sidestep the IDA's audit."

Zhoel's HGU chimed with an incoming approval from the permitting office. A second chime quickly followed, notifying him of the official's contact details. Amazed by how easily government officials could be bought, he nodded in gratitude. "Thank you."

"I've forwarded the necessary documents," the official said with a wink. "Please be advised, however, that your original deadline to depart Earth remains in effect."

The hologram flickered out, and Zhoel's shoulders relaxed.

Lila squeezed his hand again. "How long do you have?"

"I've got two days left on my visa." The impending deadline weighed on him like gravity on Hollox Prime.

"But that's Christmas Eve!" Her sudden dismay clanged across his Iki'i. "You can't leave before Christmas!"

He pulled her close and pressed a kiss to her forehead, thinking about her mother's reaction to him being present during the important holiday. "I doubt your family feels the same way."

Lila pulled back, her eyes flashing with determination. "Don't worry about Mom. My brother's girlfriend is coming for Christmas, so I can bring a…" Her voice wavered for a moment before she continued, "A guest, too."

Before he could respond, his HGU chimed with a message from an unknown sender. Frowning, he opened it and discovered another request for access to the beta version of his app.

"What is it?" Lila asked.

Reading aloud, he said, "I'm interested in your intergalactic dating and travel app. I heard about it from a friend in the permit office." He let out a breath and smiled. "It sounds like our official passed on the information."

"Is that good?"

"Sort of." He rubbed his forehead. "Plenty of Kirenai are intrigued by Earth culture. But I don't have any humans on the app for them to date yet."

"Well, that's easy." Lila reached over to her nightstand and retrieved her phone, flopping back on the rumpled blankets. "If there's a silver lining to being trapped in a small town, it's knowing everyone else who's trapped with you. I can shortlist some women who might be up for a date or two." She looked up from her phone, eyes narrowed. "We are just talking dating, right? Not sex?"

"Any sex must be consensual." He smiled at her lying comfortably on the bed they'd just shared, thinking how lucky he was. "I want to focus on interpersonal and cultural interactions rather than finding mates."

Lila nodded and returned her attention to her phone. "Well, most of the single women I know are sick of the limited dating pool. If there's a chance to meet a charming alien—like you—I think they'll be intrigued."

"Charming?" Zhoel raised an eyebrow, leaning closer. "I don't recall you being charmed when we first met."

Lila rolled her eyes with a grin. "Yeah, well, when I first saw you, I thought, 'Oh great, another one of Nana's setups.' But now…" Her voice softened, her gaze meeting his. "Now, I see the real you, Zhoel. And I want to help make this work—not just for the business, but for us, too…"

His heart swelled with gratitude and something deeper, an emotion that filled every crevice of his soul. He leaned forward, brushing a tender kiss against her forehead. In that moment, he dared to hope that she would agree to become his mate, that this bond they were forming would become more solid than any business venture. "Thank you, Lila."

The moment lingered between them, the warmth of her smile and the closeness of her body making him yearn for more. But there was still so much to do—and so little time.

Lila cleared her throat and pulled away. "All right, let's get a list together. I'm thinking of some friends who'd be game for joining a new dating app. Maybe Kylie… or even… Ann."

Zhoel tilted his head, recalling the lively blonde from the cafe. "Ann? The one who tried to kiss me under the mistletoe?"

Lila's eyes sparkled with amusement. "That's the one. She's always on the hunt for a new man. She'll be delighted to date men from another planet. Hmmm, I wonder if she's at the coffee shop now."

Zhoel nodded, though he had his doubts. "If you think she'd be a good match for someone, then it's worth a try."

"We'd better hurry while the breakfast crowd's still there." Lila hopped from the bed and headed toward the door. "Grab your shirt and let's go." Without waiting for him to pull it on, she flung open the door and froze.

Diane stood on the other side, one hand raised in readiness to knock. Her eyes narrowed as they flicked from her daughter to Zhoel's naked chest. "Why is he in your room, Lila?"

## 11

Mom's expression went from startled to furious as fast as the touchdown of a tornado. She jabbed a finger at Zhoel's still-bare chest. "I knew we shouldn't have trusted you!" Looking over her shoulder, she shouted, "Adam! Adam, get up here!"

"No, Mom, stop!" Lila grabbed her mom's hand. "I want Zhoel here. I asked him in."

Her mother yanked her into the hallway, attempting to wedge herself between Zhoel and Lila. "He's obviously using his alien powers to coerce you."

Lila dug in her heels, refusing to budge. "He's not coercing me and he's not here to do anything nefarious. Just because he's an alien is no reason to suspect him of bad intentions."

Mom gave up tugging and crossed her arms. "I'd have a problem with this situation even if he was human. You barely know each other." Her gaze on Zhoel could've shot laser beams. "We don't know his customs, or... or anything. How can you trust him?"

Dad's voice floated up from downstairs. "Are you calling me, Diane?"

"It's fine, Dad!" Lila called back.

Zhoel had shrugged into his shirt and now raised both hands as if in surrender. "I understand your concern, Mrs. Carson. My arrival has not gone how I planned. I came here looking for a business partner. I didn't expect to find something more. Please believe my intentions are genuine. I care for Lila more than anything and would never do anything to harm her or her loved ones."

"I need you to trust my judgment on this," Lila interjected softly, then glanced shyly at Zhoel and added, "He means a lot to me." Her mind wasn't yet ready to accept the whole fated mates thing, but her heart already felt bound.

Mom took a deep breath and let it out shakily. "You're my baby girl and I only want what's best for you. I don't want to see you make mistakes like your sister did."

Down the hall, the squeak of door hinges drew Lila's attention just before Sara hissed, "Mom, I told you not to say anything!"

Lila frowned. "What did she do?"

Her mother's features crumpled on the verge of tears. "Your sister is getting a divorce."

Sara huffed and shut the door with a heavy thud.

"But they just had a baby!" Lila knew her sister had been struggling, but hadn't realized things had gotten so bad.

"Yes, and the divorce papers insist she has to stay in Illinois because of the kids. She can't even come back home." Mom's voice cracked. "Sara is far enough away. I don't want you to end up trapped on another planet."

The thrill of possibly traveling to another planet made Lila's breath catch, but the sadness in her mother's eyes dulled that excitement. Clearly, Mom didn't want both her daughters' lives changing so quickly. "We're nowhere near making choices like that, but Zhoel and I are moving forward on a business deal regardless of our... personal interactions." Lila reached out and took her mom's hands, holding them tight. "I promise this won't stress you or Dad. Let us handle things. You know I've always wanted to travel, and this may just give me that chance."

Mom searched Lila's face for a long, quiet moment, then, as if finding something she needed, pulled her daughter into a hug. "I suppose it is probably time we started handing things over to you kids." Squeezing as if she never intended to let go, Mom glared at Zhoel over Lila's shoulder. "If you hurt her, I promise I'll make you regret it."

"You don't need to worry, Mrs. Carson." Zhoel's voice warmed the air with reassurance.

Mom kissed Lila's cheek and released her, turning and walking back down the hallway.

Lila let out a slow breath, shoulders sagging with relief. She glanced at her sister's closed door, and briefly considered knocking, but Josh's muffled voice on the other side stopped her. Sara wouldn't want to talk with the kids around.

Heart aching, Lila mumbled, "Poor Sara," as she led Zhoel down the stairs.

Zhoel paused on the bottom step, looking up. "Why would anyone want to leave his mate, especially when they have produced offspring together?"

"People divorce for lots of reasons. Sara's husband is gone a lot for work, and she's wondered if he's been cheating for a long time now." Lila scowled. Her mom's concern about Zhoel abandoning her lingered in the back of her mind, and she gave him a sideways look. "You say Kirenai mate for life, but does that mean couples are happy forever? Or just stuck with each other?"

Zhoel nodded thoughtfully. "Even mated couples can experience hardship, but I trust we can work through whatever challenges we face together and come out stronger in the end."

Lila laughed uncomfortably. "Slow down, Zhoel. I'm not quite ready for wedding vows."

He smiled, eyes dancing with an undeniable affection that made her heart flutter. "As you wish. Are you ready to go?"

He helped her shrug into her coat before putting on his own. She grabbed her purse and stepped out into the crisp morning air. Despite the recent tense interaction with her mother, the pale blue sky felt light with promise and the thrill of something new. She took Zhoel's hand and walked down the snowy path, heading toward the cafe.

They walked in comfortable silence, boots crunching on the icy sidewalk. Being with Zhoel felt nice, like they were on the same page in a way that didn't require words. Lila felt more optimistic than she'd felt in a very long time. They had faced her mother—together—and they had made it through. Now they were going to save the trucking company and get his business started, assuming Ann was as willing to join Zhoel's app as she hoped.

The bell above the cafe door chimed as they entered, and the warm, bitter scent of coffee enveloped them. Lila's stomach rumbled, and she glanced at Zhoel with embarrassment.

He gave her a knowing smile. "We worked up quite an appetite. Allow me to order this time," he said, striding toward the counter where the barista was helping another customer.

The cafe patrons watched Zhoel curiously, but with fewer open-mouthed stares than yesterday. Lila spotted Ann sitting with two of her friends, all eyes on Zhoel. Their appreciative stares made Lila's chest burn with jealousy, but she quickly reminded herself of her bedroom last night. *Zhoel is mine.*

Standing taller, she smiled and wove her way between the tables toward Ann. "Hey, Ann." She nodded at the other women. "Kylie, Steph. Mind if I join you?"

"Ooh, should we make room for your alien friend, too?" Ann scooted over and slid a vacant chair from a nearby table into place beside her.

Lila pulled a fifth chair up to the table, then pointedly took the chair next to Ann. "Yes. In fact, we want to talk to you about something." She looked toward Zhoel, who was speaking animatedly with the barista. "It's about a dating app he's been working on."

"Dating app? For aliens?" Kylie asked, one manicured brow arched in curiosity.

Ann tapped a polished nail against the tabletop. "He turned me down with the mistletoe. Now he's into dating?"

"Not Zhoel himself," Lila clarified. "He has some beta testers who are interested in coming to Earth."

"If they're as hot as he is, sign me up!" Steph said, gaze riveted on Zhoel's backside.

Lila tried not to scowl. "I haven't seen the candidates yet, but probably. Every Kirenai I've ever seen on the Internet is gorgeous." She thought about the pale alien from the permit office and added, "And there are other aliens to choose from, too. They're all really interesting."

Zhoel arrived with two steaming cups and set one in front of Lila, filling the air with the scent of warm mocha. "I also ordered something called bagels which will be ready when they come out of the toaster."

He pulled the empty chair close to Lila's and sat, making the other women at the table grin and give each other knowing looks. Steph mumbled, "Go Lila."

Face heating, Lila cleared her throat. "Thanks, Zhoel. I was just telling them about your app. Is there a way they can get a glimpse of the dating pool?"

"Of course." Zhoel pulled his holographic device from his pocket and set it on the table.

Once the women got over their curiosity about the device, he scrolled through several holograms, mostly ubiquitously handsome Kirenai. Lila also recognized the permitting official in one and a gray alien with a craggy face and horns in another. "My app will allow you to talk with them prior to agreeing to a date. Once you pick someone, we can arrange travel, accommodations, and locations for dates. As beta users, you may not find your perfect match right away, but you will be helping me refine the interface."

Ann traced a finger through the hologram of a Kirenai with thick eyebrows and broody eyes. "Sign me up. I'm an expert at first dates."

*Not so expert at second dates,* Lila thought, though maybe this app would help change that.

Glad to have Ann's attention on someone other than Zhoel, Lila said, "Thank you, Ann."

Kylie nodded. "I'm up for meeting handsome aliens. Count me in."

"Me, too," added Steph.

"Wonderful!" Zhoel said.

As he showed the women how to access the app via their phones, Lila's spirits lifted. For the first time in a long while, she felt like things were falling into place. They spent the next hour brainstorming ideas, sharing laughs, and talking about how to make the app successful. Ann and the others had advice for everything from lodging to meals, surprising Lila with the thoughtful ways they suggested sharing human culture with extraterrestrial men. *I guess not everything Ann does is lewd or self-serving.*

But as the conversation continued, Lila felt more and more out of place. Kylie asked about possibly taking her date to a play in the city, and Steph took the idea and expanded it into international travel.

"Humans have different cultures all over the world," said Steph, mirroring Lila's own desire to travel. "Wouldn't it be fun if the couple got to experience a new culture together?"

Zhoel was excited about the prospect and started taking notes on his holographic device. "A shared experience like that could help create strong bonds."

Lila sat back in her chair, slowly growing more and more despondent. She'd wondered how her family's trucking business could fit into Zhoel's business model before, but now it was becoming clear that it didn't. What did trucking have to do with picking the best lodging or choosing a venue for a romantic dinner? Transportation wasn't the troublesome part of dating. What Zhoel needed was a vacation planner. Not a bookkeeper for a failing company. *Not me.*

A lump formed in her throat as the truth settled in her mind. She looked at Zhoel, his eyes flashing with excitement as Steph talked about having a date at a salsa dancing class in Puerto Rico. She never would've thought of that. Or a stroll through London's botanical gardens like Kylie suggested. *I've barely ventured past a traditional dinner and a movie date.* Who was she to think she could help get Zhoel's app off the ground?

Zhoel squeezed her hand, saying something about going on a food tour. Lila nodded, forcing a smile. But deep down, the seed of a difficult decision had taken root. *I can't partner with Zhoel.* He deserved the best chance at success, and she couldn't let anything —not even her need to save her family's business— hold him back.

## 12

Zhoel's mocha had grown cold as he listened to the women talk about dating. At the moment, he was entranced by Steph's story about a date at something called a "tailgate party," though he was still unsure how it had anything to do with gates or tails. Human traditions were fascinating.

"It's most fun when the weather's nice and you can do it in the parking lot," Steph was saying. "We grill burgers and blast music to get hyped before the game. Some guys get really wild, painting themselves with the team colors. Then we all go watch the game."

Ann leaned close and looped one arm through his. "This time of year, the parties are cozier and held indoors. There's a game on TV tomorrow night if you're interested in coming over to my place."

"Thank you, but I'm spending tomorrow night with Lila." Politely withdrawing his arm, Zhoel turned toward Lila and realized her chair was empty. He glanced around the cafe, noting the tables were no longer crowded. Through the large plate-glass windows, snow drifted lazily from the sky. He'd been here longer than he'd realized. "Lila?"

"She waved goodbye a little while ago," said Kylie.

He vaguely recalled Lila mumbling something about putting her cup away. Cursing himself for not noticing she hadn't returned, Zhoel rose and stuffed his HGU into his pocket. "Thank you for all your help, ladies. We'll be in touch again in a day or two to coordinate your first dates."

"Don't go yet!" said Ann. "We have a lot more ideas to share."

"I'll have to take you up on that another time." Zhoel took his unfinished mug to the counter before heading for the exit.

As he stepped into the cold, his mind raced, wondering why Lila had left without him. He didn't recall her saying anything about another obligation today. On the street, he saw no sign of her. Perhaps she went to tell her mother about their success?

His steps lightened as he pictured Lila waiting for him at her home, ready to celebrate. He was more certain than ever she'd agree to be his mate after today's success. Tomorrow they'd spend Christmas Eve with her family, then he'd teleport back to his ship and arrange for Lila to join him on board. Everything felt right. He had people joining the app and now felt his permanent permit to conduct business on Earth would be approved without a hitch. They could integrate Lila's trucking company into his business model, and with her by his side, they'd open his app to every corner of her planet. Maybe even branch out to include dates on other planets someday.

Feeling like he was heading to his own home, he turned toward the Carson family house. Snowflakes coated the sidewalk ahead in a sheet of pristine white. He traced a human symbol that Kylie had shown him on a patch of sidewalk—two rounded hills that reminded him of the luscious curve of

Lila's ass, with a V below that reminded him of the sweet well between her legs. No wonder humans use this symbol for love. Perhaps he should incorporate it into his company logo. He grinned and continued on.

When he reached the house, he trotted up the porch steps and knocked on the door, fingers itching to grasp the knob and burst right in. A few moments later, Lila appeared, her eyes shadowed with something he couldn't quite place. Immediately, his Iki'i felt off—their connection distant, muted. The elation he'd been feeling sank like a balloon losing air.

"Lila?" He reached for her, but she stopped him with one hand. He frowned. "What's the matter?"

She slipped outside and pulled the door closed behind her, crossing her arms against the cold. In a soft voice almost lost in the stillness of the falling snow, she said, "We need to talk."

His throat tightened. "Of course. About what?"

"I don't think our partnership is a good fit," she said. "Not for the business. Not… for us."

The ground seemed to tilt. "Why would you think this?" he asked.

"I worried about it before, shifting Carson Family Trucking's focus from freight to people. But after talking with Ann and the others, I realized you're going to need more than transportation—you need logistics and coordination across the globe. We're a small-town company with a local focus. You need a partner with bigger…" her lip caught in her teeth, as if struggling for the words, "…international connections."

He moved closer. "Hopefully someday, yes, but right now, all the beta testers are here in Bloomington. Your business and mine will grow and expand together." He reached out and touched her shoulder. "Lila, we can make this work."

"You were so caught up listening to Ann and the others, so caught up in the excitement of expansion and ideas, you didn't even realize I had left." She blinked, eyes glistening before she looked away. "Your dreams are much bigger than this town, Zhoel. You need to travel, and I'm tied down here."

"No, you're not." He smiled, taking her chin to turn

her to face him. "We'll just hire someone to take over your job—"

He felt the remainder of their tenuous connection slip like sand through his fingers as she jerked away. "Why do men assume I can just abandon my job to someone else? I'm not just 'some hire' and I do more than bookkeeping. I've worked hard to build our company. We can't afford to just pay people to take over."

"I'll pay for it out of my budget. You're my mate, and I need you by my side. You'll continue to help build your family's business, just in a different role." Zhoel tried to use his Iki'i to reach her, to feel her emotions, but it was as if a wall had gone up between them.

"I have to stay. You have to go." Lila took a step back, one hand resting on the doorknob. "I'm sorry, Zhoel. I hope your app succeeds. You have something amazing to offer the universe. But we're not mates, and I don't see a way our businesses can intersect."

Before he could say anything else, she opened the door and slipped inside. The click of the latch echoed in the silence, leaving Zhoel alone and staring at the closed door.

A bitter gust of wind eddied snow across the porch, coldness sinking into his bones. How had this happened? The future he'd envisioned, the life he'd dreamed of with Lila—all of it had dissipated like his breath in the wind, leaving nothing but chill emptiness in its wake.

He realized his hand was hovering just shy of the door handle. Everything inside him screamed to chase after her, to make her see the future he envisioned—one that was filled with her laughter, her presence by his side, the fulfillment of both their dreams. Instead, he stepped back, legs heavy and chest hollow.

*My Iki'i has failed me again.*

He should've known what she was feeling. Been able to stave off her concerns. The crushing disappointment filling him now was worse than when he'd failed his father. He thought she'd been excited to travel. Excited to expand her family's business. *Do I even know what her dreams really are?*

Turning, Zhoel stumbled down the porch steps, heart aching with every beat. He paused at the bottom, looking back at the house for a long, long time. The window to the living room glowed softly, and he could almost hear the echoes of laughter from the previous night—the comfort of a family he'd hoped to join. He'd misread the situation and lost his chance—just like he always did.

A car rushed past on the street behind him, and a lonely dog barked in the distance. The ashy scent of smoke drifted from someone's fireplace with no hint of warmth. It had been foolish to think he could build a life with someone like Lila, that he could truly belong to anyone. The universe was vast, and maybe he was destined to roam it alone, an outsider forever looking in.

He turned away from the house and began to walk, feet shushing through the fresh snow. The streets of Bloomington were quiet, and a chill breeze bit through his clothes, but he barely noticed. He eventually found himself at the edge of the skating pond. The rink was empty now, the surface hidden by snow. The memory of his time with her lingered like a dream—how happy they'd been, the way she'd looked at him, full of warmth and joy. He could still feel the press of her lips, the thrill that had coursed through his veins, the certainty that she was his.

For the first time since he'd come to Earth, Zhoel felt truly lost.

He dropped onto a bench at the edge of the pond, burying his face in his hands. His Iki'i thrummed with sorrow, Lila's absence a deep, aching void that he didn't know how to fill. Even the success of his app held no joy. Earth held nothing for him if he couldn't experience it with her.

Maybe it was time to accept that he didn't belong here—that he didn't belong anywhere. He was just an alien, a stranger who had dared to hope for too much.

He reached into his pocket for his HGU so he could send his coordinates to the teleporter, but his fingers met a tangle of leaves and berries. *Mistletoe.* As he pulled it out, Ann's words returned to him: *you kiss under it for luck.* What he wouldn't do for some of that luck right now.

A slow determination rose inside him. He'd come here to learn about human culture for his business, and there was one last Christmas tradition he wanted to experience with Lila. With the mistletoe clutched tightly in one fist and his heart hammering, he began striding back toward her house.

## 13

*L*ila stood with her back against the front door for what felt like forever, an aching pit where her heart used to be. The finality of her decision, the shock in Zhoel's eyes as she'd closed the door—made her feel like she was drowning. *He's just like Craig,* she tried to tell herself, *dismissing the importance of my job and family.* Better to end things now than break her heart later when he left her behind.

She clutched her sweater over her chest, denying the heartbreak she was feeling. "I did the right thing," she whispered to herself, voice cracking as emptiness threatened to swallow her.

Josh and Emily burst from the living room and ran past, giggling with childish delight, their laughter echoing through the hallway. From the kitchen, she heard her mother clattering dishes and speaking to Sara. Remembering her sister's divorce, she squeezed her eyes shut. *I should go offer a sympathetic ear.* Pushing off the door, she stood there a moment, trying to summon the will to move.

And stood there.

She just didn't have it in her to comfort someone else. With heavy feet, she plodded upstairs to her bedroom. She couldn't wipe the look of Zhoel's despair from her mind. Was that how she'd always remember him now? He'd been so excited when he'd spoken of their future, and she'd torn it all apart.

She collapsed onto her bed, face in her pillow, only to realize it smelled like Zhoel. "Dammit."

Choking with longing, she rose and turned to face the window, gaze snagging on the stuffed rabbit Zhoel had won for her at the Christmas Carnival. It sat lopsided on her dresser, its beady eyes seeming to question her decision.

"Did I do the right thing?" she whispered thickly.

She hugged the stuffed rabbit to her chest, face buried in its plush fur. The past two days had been a magical whirlwind, a tumultuous mix of joy and fear, uncertainty and pleasure. She'd felt alive and full of hope for the future she'd always dreamed of.

But she couldn't leave; Mom couldn't run things on her own. When Lila'd taken over the books, she'd transferred everything to the computer. Then there was the fleet scheduling, safety compliance, load permitting, and so much more. *I have responsibilities here.* Yet her attempted rationalizations echoed hollow in her chest.

A knock on her door startled her, and she pressed a finger and thumb to her eyes to be sure there weren't any tears before calling out, "Yes?"

The door creaked open, and Nana Pearl peeked in, her expression soft. "Mind if I come in, sweetheart?"

Lila nodded, throat suddenly too tight to speak. This had all started because of Nana and her matchmaking. Yet Lila couldn't bring herself to be angry. Nana only wanted her to be happy, after all.

Nana entered, followed by Sara, and Lila restrained a groan when she saw Mom hovering in the doorway. *I should've just joined them in the kitchen.*

"Where's Zhoel?" Nana asked as she sat on the edge of the bed. "Is everything okay?"

*Well, crap.* This wasn't going to be about Sara's divorce. Lila shoved the stuffed rabbit back onto her dresser. "It's fine. I realized the business partnership wasn't a good fit," she said, her voice catching. "Mom was right."

Mom made a discontented noise from the doorway, and Lila avoided looking at her, afraid of the recrimination she'd find.

Sara came over and put an arm around her. "But there's more to you two than business. What happened?"

Lila met her sister's concerned gaze, feeling awful in so many ways. Here she was whining over a relationship that was barely a day old, and her sister was ending a years-long marriage. "I should be consoling you, not the other way around."

"Surprisingly, I'm more relieved than upset," Sara said, though her smile was sad. "I've been vacillating for a long time, worried about making a mistake, worried about giving up too soon. But when he asked for a divorce, I realized I've been working on our relationship alone all along." She let out a shaky breath and spoke in a near whisper, "I'm terrified, but I think it's for the best."

"It'll be okay." Lila hugged her. "We're here for you." Bitterness crept up Lila's throat. *Right here in Bloomington, like always.*

Sara nodded, her eyes misty. "I know. Honestly, once I'm ready, I might even try Zhoel's app. See what's out there."

Lila started to chuckle, but it turned into a half-sob she forced herself to swallow.

"Is he coming back?" asked Nana.

"No," Lila said.

"That's too bad," said Sara. "I was starting to like him, and you two seemed to be really hitting it off."

"We barely knew each other a day, and he was insisting I'm the one." Lila forced her voice to remain strong. "He was moving way too fast."

Nana chuckled. "Your grandad was the same way. We met at the town fair. I beat him at a shooting game, and he stared at me, all fire and frustration. I thought he'd stalk off, but he asked if I'd join him for a dance instead. We barely knew each other, but I said yes. I knew right then he was the one. When you know, you know, sweetheart."

Lila shook her head. "Zhoel needs to travel, and I can't just abandon my responsibilities here to be with him."

Mom crossed her arms, her lips pressed into a thin line. "Lila, your dad and I ran the trucking company for decades before you started working there. We can manage without you, at least for a while. You don't have to sacrifice your happiness for us."

"But that was before Dad's heart attack," Lila said. "He can't take on as much as he used to. Plus, I moved all our financials to the computer and you barely know how to turn it on."

Sara cleared her throat. "I'm going to need a job now. I can take over and do the bookkeeping from home if Mom can handle the other stuff you do."

Mom nodded. "Absolutely. Your Aunt Maggie said her boss will be retiring in a few months and mentioned needing part time work. I bet she'd be delighted to help. Between the three of us, we'll keep the business up and running."

Lila looked around at her family, her heart melting at the loving support she saw on their faces. Mom's eyes were glossy with unshed tears, and Nana's were full of love. Sara was smiling and nodding encouragement. *Could I really leave Bloomington behind to be with Zhoel?* Was that even an option anymore after how she'd treated him?

Mom stepped into the room and put one arm around each of her daughters, squeezing tightly. "We're a family. We do anything for each other." Releasing the hug, she took Lila's shoulders and turned her around so they were face-to-face. "Both of my daughters deserve happiness, and Lila, if you think your happiness is with Zhoel, you need to be with him."

Feeling shaky inside, Lila said, "This is a big decision. What if it's a mistake?"

Nana Pearl clucked her tongue. "That's what being young is all about, making mistakes. When I was your age, I made some tough choices too. I had some regrets, but most of the time, it worked out for the best. It'll be the same for you."

"You've been using your job as an excuse for too long, Lila," Mom said firmly. "Go live your life."

Sara lifted her chin. "It's time we both start living for ourselves."

They were right. Lila had been hiding behind her responsibilities, afraid of making bad choices. It was time to stop putting everyone else's needs before her own. She'd found something real with Zhoel—something that made her feel alive, and she couldn't just throw it away because she was too scared to take a risk.

Then her throat tightened. She had no way of contacting Zhoel. She'd been so hell-bent on breaking things off, she hadn't thought to ask. Had he left for his ship already? Ann and the others had his app on their phones, but Lila'd been feeling too sorry for herself to bother loading it to hers. *God, I really don't want to ask Ann to contact him for me.* She shook her head, trying to push away the fear creeping in again. Now wasn't the time to give up, or she'd live with regret for the rest of her life.

"I need to make a phone call." She reached for her phone.

Downstairs, the thud of the front door closing announced Dad's return home. His voice echoed up the stairs. "Hello? Anyone home?"

The sound of children squealing with glee and racing to greet him filled the air, and the baby started crying from Sara's room down the hall.

Sara gave Lila a quick hug before leaving to tend to her children. "Good luck."

Dad's footsteps thudded up the stairs, and he poked his head into Lila's room, his hair damp from melting snow. "Why was Zhoel standing in our driveway?"

Lila sucked in a breath. "What? He's here?"

"In the foyer. I told him to come inside and warm up." Dad shook his head. "He said something about wanting to experience a Christmas tradition."

Christmas tradition? What was he talking about? Lila's heart was pounding a thousand beats a minute as she dashed out of her room and down the stairs. Zhoel stood near the door as if afraid to take another step, his blue skin looking like ice in the overhead light. Yet his gaze was anything but icy. He lifted one hand above his head. "For luck before I go?"

She frowned, then noticed the sprig of leaves and white berries pinched between his fingers.

Mistletoe. *He wants a kiss.* A laugh burbled up from her chest, and she moved toward him. "Zhoel, I—"

Her words were cut off by his mouth coming down to cover hers. She sucked in a breath, unexpected heat flaring through her. She leaned into the kiss, and as if he'd been waiting for permission, he wrapped his free arm around her middle and crushed her against his chest.

Surrendering to the moment, she let all her worries melt away. Zhoel was her mate. She knew it now with all her heart.

She slid her arms around his neck and inhaled deeply, taking in his sandalwood scent. His tongue danced and explored, gentle yet passionate, each touch sending waves of joy and desire throughout her body. It was a kiss that spoke volumes, conveying unspoken desires and a depth of emotion that left her breathless.

Eventually, he broke the kiss long enough to murmur, "I thought you'd turn me away."

"I'm glad you came back."

He pressed his forehead to hers. "I'm not going anywhere, Lila. I love you."

*Love?* And she realized that insane as it seemed, she loved him, too. In a voice trembling with emotion, she whispered, "Me, too, Zhoel. I love you, too."

His breath hitched, and he pulled back to look at her, his eyes full of incredulity. Then he lowered the mistletoe and stared at it. "This stuff really is lucky."

## 14

Zhoel spent most of Christmas Eve signing contracts with Lila, finalizing the business permit for Earth, and joining her for some last-minute shopping. Since they planned to leave together before his visa expired tonight, her family was going to open presents early, and Lila was fretting over something called 'stocking stuffers.'

Sauntering down Main Street hand-in-hand, Zhoel and Lila peered through store windows while shoppers gawked at him, though most smiled and nodded when Lila greeted them. He regretted not having more time to spend exploring Bloomington before his visa expired, but he knew he and Lila would be back.

They entered a small store filled with the scent of sugar and chocolate. Shelves lined the store from floor to ceiling, stacked with jars, bins and packages of multi-colored sweets. While Lila picked out and paid for a few purchases, Zhoel perused the fascinating wares: striped white and red 'candy canes,' bite-sized lumps of filled chocolate called 'truffles,' and multitudes of squishy 'gummies' in every shape imaginable.

As they left the shop, Lila offered him something she called a peanut butter cup. The shape reminded him of a pie rather than a cup, but Zhoel took a bite, savoring the slightly salty filling inside the sweet outer shell. "Why does your family put food in their socks for the holiday? It seems like an unsanitary practice."

Lila burst out laughing, shaking her head. "Not socks. Stockings. And they're not for wearing. They just hang by the fireplace to be filled by Santa."

"I see." He sucked the sweetness from his teeth. "But you are filling them, not Santa."

She smiled and took his arm, leading him down the street. "Santa isn't real. Not anymore, at least. He's just a myth we tell children to bring them joy and encourage them to be good throughout the year. Though often that joy extends to more than just children."

"Ah, I see. On the planet Valoren, they have a tradition where children place small baskets of fruit outside their doors at night. In the morning, they find the fruit replaced by memory crystals providing knowledge from the spirits of their ancestors. It's meant to show that the family is being watched over and protected."

"Wow, that sounds amazing. I can't wait to visit places like that with you." Lila beamed up at him, and he bent to brush a kiss across her forehead.

"Are there more stocking stuffers you need to buy?" he asked.

"No, I think I've bought more than enough. Let's get home. I need to help Mom with dinner."

Zhoel was still a little anxious about integrating with her family, particularly her mother and brother, but Lila seemed to believe everything would be all right. Hopefully, the gift he had planned for Lila's family would be approved and arrive in time for the gathering. Alien technology was highly restricted on Earth, and he prayed that the partnership he'd signed between his company and Lila's was enough to provide an exemption in this instance.

They entered Lila's home to mouthwatering aromas coming from the kitchen. Lila's father, brother, and uncle sat in the living room watching a screen with what appeared to be teams of wide-shouldered humans attempting to maintain control of an elongated ball.

"Why don't you join the guys watching football while I help in the kitchen?" Lila said, nudging him toward the living room.

He didn't need his Iki'i to tell him she wanted time alone with her mother, so he did as she suggested, taking a seat on one end of the sofa. Recalling Steph's description of this game, he said, "Thank you for allowing me to join your tailgate party."

Tom shot him a confused look, but Adam pointed to several unopened bottles on the table in front of the sofa. "Help yourself to a beer."

Smiling at the opportunity to share another human tradition, he popped open a bottle and sat back to observe the game. The slightly bitter beverage was pleasant on his tongue, and he was still trying to understand the concept of *football* when Lila came to announce dinner.

Everyone moved into the dining room where a large roasted bird dominated the center of the table, its golden skin glistening under the lights. So many new and delightful scents filled the room, he couldn't wait to try each and every dish. As he loaded his plate, Lila nudged him and laughed. "Make sure you save room for pie."

The meal was fantastic, and the promised pie was bliss, a fruity concoction of apples and spices topped by sweet frozen cream. But even better than the food was the laughter and love infiltrating his Iki'i. Sara shared stories about her kids, and Nana recounted past Christmases. Lila's father cracked jokes that had everyone—including Zhoel—laughing along. Once in a while, his Iki'i caught a melancholy note from Lila, and he'd squeeze her hand under the table, knowing that despite her excitement for their future journeys together, she was still sad about leaving her family behind.

After dinner, they gathered in the living room to open gifts. Dad and Nana sat in their usual recliners, with everyone else taking spots on the sofas. Josh and Emily crowded up against the presents beneath the tree.

"Do you really have to leave before Christmas, Lila?" asked Simone, leaning forward to peer toward Lila.

Lila nodded, shrugging. "Zhoel's permit runs out in a few hours. We have to go or they might arrest him."

"Nobody's arresting *you*, Lila," said Tom with a scowl. "You could still spend one last holiday with your family."

Guilt rolled through Zhoel, and he looked at Lila. "You can stay if you like."

"Heck, no," Lila insisted. "I need to be with you in case the IDA gives you more trouble. Plus, I'm a little nervous about the teleportation thing. I'd rather my first time be with you at my side."

He was glad she wanted to come with him, but also understood what it meant that she'd be missing the holiday. That's why he was trying to arrange this gift. He checked his HGU again, growing anxious, but still no approval.

As the family exchanged more presents, Lila leaned her head against his shoulder, lacing her fingers through his. It was clear how much she loved her family, and how much they loved her in return. Lila gave Tom a book on classic cars, his face lighting up as he flipped through the pages. Simone handed Lila a small box containing a pair of earrings shaped like tiny passports. "If we'd known you'd be traveling to space, we'd have looked for UFOs," said Simone with a laugh.

"They're perfect," insisted Lila, placing them in her ears.

Nana gave Lila a hand-knit sweater that she immediately wrapped around her shoulders. She rose and gave Nana a hug. "This is perfect. Thank you."

Zhoel was surprised when Lila's dad handed him a box. "For me?"

Adam nodded. "Sorry we didn't have more time to get to know each other before you have to leave."

Inside was a small snow globe depicting a miniature scene of Bloomington. Zhoel grinned and shook it, watching the snow fall around the small buildings. He held it out to Lila. "The first in our collection."

Tears glistened in her eyes, but she smiled and nodded. "Thanks, Dad."

Zhoel's HGU chimed, and he quickly checked the message, heart thundering with anticipation. "It's here," he said, standing.

Lila looked up at him, curiosity brightening her eyes. "What's here?"

"You'll see. I'll be right back."

He hurried to the front door and opened it. A small drone hovered just outside, two square silver boxes held securely in its grip. The drone released the boxes into Zhoel's hands and quickly zipped away into the night.

Zhoel turned to find everyone standing in the entry to the living room, watching him expectantly. He found Lila's mom and stepped toward her. "This is for your family. For you, especially."

Diane's eyes widened as she carefully took the box he offered. She opened it to reveal a small, glowing orb nestled inside. "What is it?"

"This one's for you, Lila." He held the other box out. She opened it and removed a matching globe. Zhoel continued, "These are modified HGUs, specially calibrated so you can talk to each other no matter how far away we are."

He showed them how to operate the orbs, bringing the respective holograms to life. Everyone laughed as Lila cracked a joke and the holographic Lila mimicked Lila's actions and words.

"Thank you," Diane said, surprising Zhoel with a hug. "This means more than you could ever know."

Zhoel's Iki'i swelled, enveloped by the love and gratitude emanating from Lila's entire family. "I just wanted you all to know how much Lila means to me. And that I understand how much all of you mean to her—to us."

His HGU pinged, alerting him it was time to go. "I'm afraid our time's up."

"Wait," said Diane, hurrying to the Christmas tree. She pulled a long flat box from beneath the boughs and thrust it toward Zhoel. "One last gift."

Touched, Zhoel tore off the red wrapping and opened the box. Inside was a black jacket with the Carson Family Trucking logo stitched across the back.

Before he could say thank you, Lila flung herself against her mom in a hug. "Oh, Mom, that's so sweet."

Diane's face pinkened, and she shrugged. "Well, if he's going to be part of the family, he needs the proper attire."

Zhoel stared at the jacket, his chest tightening with emotion. He'd spent so long feeling like an outsider, always wandering, never belonging. Now this simple piece of clothing felt like a symbol of everything he'd always wanted. A family. A place to call home. He blinked rapidly, trying to keep his emotions in check as he put it on, feeling its warmth wrap around him.

"I'm honored," he said, his voice thick.

While Lila shared a tearful goodbye with her family, Adam gave Zhoel a firm handshake and a pat on the back. "We can't wait to hear all about your adventures."

Lila's mother clung to her daughter, rasping, "I'm going to miss you."

Tears coating her cheeks, Lila returned the hug, but she smiled at Zhoel over her mom's shoulder, letting him know it was all okay.

"Come here, Zhoel," said Nana, pulling him down to plant a solid kiss on his cheek. "I know you'll take good care of my granddaughter."

"I will, Nana. And we'll come back to visit often."

Tom gave Lila a quick hug, muttering, "The office won't be the same without you, sis."

Lila punched him lightly in the arm. "Yeah, who's going to wash your greasy handprints off the coffee machine now?" She turned and hugged her sister. "Love you. Good luck keeping everyone in line."

Josh grabbed Zhoel's hand and tugged him toward the door. "C'mon. I wanna see you teleport."

Zhoel laughed. "Hold on, buddy." He patted the child on the head, then retrieved Lila's enormous suitcase from the base of the stairs. "Ready, Lila?"

She gave Zhoel a tremulous smile. "Ready as I'll ever be."

He took her hand, heart swelling with love for this amazing woman who was willing to leave everything she knew to be with him. Together, they descended the porch steps and turned to look up at her family. "I love you guys," called Lila.

"We'll be back soon," Zhoel added before turning to look at Lila. "But right now, I'm going to show Lila the stars."

# 15

Teleportation turned out to be anti-climactic, but being on a spaceship was not. Lila stood next to Zhoel on the observation deck of his ship, staring through a curved dome at a breathtaking number of stars. The metallic floor reflected the constellations, making her feel as if they were floating amidst the heavens themselves. Earth's curve formed a thick crescent above their heads, half in darkness, half in light, the blues and greens of oceans and land bright against the darkness of space.

A small pang shot through her chest as she realized she was following her dreams differently than she'd ever imagined. Instead of strolling along the Seine in

Paris, she'd be walking on the soil of other planets. Instead of gawking at the skyscrapers in New York, she'd be sightseeing across the Milky Way. While the new options were exciting, she felt a loss she hadn't expected. Seeing other places on Earth had always been her dream.

"Look, that's Australia." She pointed toward the planet's horizon. "I always wanted to tour the Outback."

"Well, why don't we?" said Zhoel, adjusting a setting on a pedestal in the center of the deck. The ship rotated, moving her view of Earth to eye level. "We can go as soon as our permit to return to Earth gets approved."

Lila turned a questioning glance on him. Ambient light from the pedestal's console flickered across his blue skin. "Don't we need to spend our time marketing the app on other planets?"

He smiled and wrapped an arm around her shoulders. "The app is already selling itself. Our friend in the permitting office is apparently spreading the word, and we've gotten over a hundred applicants on the waiting list in the past solar day. We need to market on Earth now so they have dates and arrange logistics all over your planet. Why not start in Australia? We'll move on to the rest of the galaxy when the time comes."

Tears prickled her eyes, and she turned to fling her arms around his neck. "I love you, Zhoel. I can't believe I almost let you go."

He pulled her close, his breath warm in her hair. In a low voice, he asked, "Does that mean you've decided about the mate bond?"

Heat flooded her entire body as she recalled their most recent discussion when he'd described how a Kirenai mate bond worked during lovemaking, a joining that went beyond physical, merging them emotionally and spiritually. She already felt a deep and unexplainable connection with Zhoel, but knowing there was more—something deeper they could share—was both exhilarating and terrifying.

There wasn't a rush, but like Nana said, when you know, you know. She looked into Zhoel's eyes, pouring all the love she felt into that gaze. "I'm ready to share my life with you."

Zhoel's smile was radiant, his eyes returning the love she was feeling tenfold. He leaned in, capturing her lips in a tender kiss before taking her hand and leading her deeper into the ship. The ship's interior still amazed her, with organic curves and softly glowing walls. They reached a huge, circular chamber with screens that looked out over a gorgeous alien landscape. A lush forest of blue and purple trees spread out below them with fantastically curved spires she assumed must be buildings poking from the canopy. Two plush armchairs sat as if looking out on a lanai, and on the opposite side of the room sat a gilded vanity and a darkly polished armoire. In the center of the room stood what appeared to be a four-poster bed covered by a rich maroon comforter and white pillows.

"Is this your bedroom?" she asked.

"Our bedroom, yes. I designed it based on information from some of Earth's most opulent hotel rooms."

She smiled at the eclectic collection, doubting she'd ever see a hotel on Earth like this one. "I've never been to a fancy hotel. Thank you."

Zhoel turned and cupped her face in both hands, looking deep into her eyes. "You are my mate, Lila

Carson. I plan to explore a lot of new things with you."

They kissed again, his hands moving down her throat and over her shoulders, sending shivers of anticipation down her spine. He pushed aside the neckline of her sweater, feathering kisses along her throat while she roamed her palms over the hard planes of his chest. She deftly opened the buttons of his shirt and pushed it away so she could feel his skin, loving the slight sprinkle of hair over his chest.

He stopped his kisses and pulled her sweater over her head, gaze roaming her breasts a moment before he lifted his hands to cup them around her lace bra. "So beautiful."

Her nipples tightened as his thumbs brushed the lace, anticipation rocketing down her belly to settle like an ache between her legs. She tweaked his nipples in return, grinning when the tiny blue buds hardened under her touch. Leaning forward, she licked one, biting it gently before moving to do the same to the other.

Making an indistinct sound of pleasure, he skimmed his hands across her back, flicking open her bra and freeing the straps from her shoulders. She let it drop to the floor and straightened, breathing shakily.

"Are you nervous?" he asked, looking into her eyes.

She nodded. "A little. But I'm more excited than anything."

He smiled, taking her hand and leading her to the bed. "We don't have to rush anything. We have all the time in the universe."

She sat on the edge of the mattress, pulse like a drum in her ears. Zhoel knelt in front of her, taking off her boots gently, his hands warm against her skin. He looked up at her, his eyes filled with love and reassurance. Lila reached out, running a hand along his angular face. His skin was warm and smooth, with a hint of roughened stubble along his jawline. She leaned down and kissed him, her fingers tangling in his hair.

Zhoel's hands slid feather-light up her legs until they reached the waistband of her jeans. He pushed her gently back against the mattress, still kissing her as he unbuttoned them. She lifted her hips, helping him push her jeans and panties down. His mouth left hers, trailing along her throat and down her chest while he slowly slid the garments downward. He circled one of her nipples with his tongue, breath hot against her skin, then kissed lower, down the front of her thighs, past her knees, before finally tugging them free. His touch felt reverent, his hands and mouth caressing her skin as if it were something precious.

He stroked her feet, rubbing his thumbs along the arches, then worked his way back up her body, massaging and kissing the insides of her legs as he went. Each touch made her tremble with anticipation, her breath shuddering and heartbeat thundering in her ears. He eased her thighs open, exposing her center to his questing tongue. A hot, wet thrust parted her slit and slid along her inner folds.

Gasping, she flexed her hips, and Zhoel slid his hands under her ass, holding her steady as he latched onto her clit and suckled. Pleasure spiraled through her, and she grasped the comforter. He flicked the sensitive nub with increasing pressure, building her rising need into a crescendo that crested and broke, sending her shuddering into release.

When her orgasm subsided, he stood, his gaze never leaving hers as he removed his pants. The defined muscles of his abs guided her attention to the thick shaft jutting from between his thighs. It seemed to pulse, the smooth head catching the light like the sheen of satin.

"I want to see your mating rod," she said, her breath husky. He'd told her he'd been keeping it from her until she was ready.

He nodded and knelt on the mattress between her legs. In a rough voice, he said, "Touch me."

Eyes glued to his shaft, she circled the thick girth, gliding downward to the base. He groaned and put a hand on her shoulder to steady himself as a smaller rod emerged from beneath his cock. She exhaled in awe, opening her thumb to stroke the bullet-shaped appendage.

"Is this it?" she whispered, her insides trembling with anticipation.

"Yes." His hips were making tiny thrusting motions against her as if out of his control. "I don't trust my Iki'i. Tell me how you want it."

She stroked the bullet-shaped rod, delighted when he shuddered and groaned again. He'd explained the appendage could be merged into his cock or used separately for her pleasure. "I think I might like to try it separate."

A feral growl escaped Zhoel's lips, and he pressed her back to the mattress. His kiss was ravenous, tongue exploring every crevice of her mouth. She tasted her own arousal on his lips, a salty-sweet reminder of where his mouth had just been, and her heart pounded hard in response.

He wrapped one hand around the back of her neck and plunged his tongue in and out, mimicking the act they were both craving. With his other hand, he reached between their bodies, grasping his cock and rubbing the velvety tip against her slick entrance, spreading her wetness and teasing her mercilessly. With each stroke, his finger brushed over her ass, each pass pressing deeper into the tight opening and heightening her arousal. She'd engaged in ass-play a couple of times, but had never anticipated it with such excitement.

Slowly, torturously, he slid his cock into her pussy, filling and stretching her until she thought she might burst from the pleasure. She lifted her hips to meet him, clawing his back with need. "Please, Zhoel," she whimpered.

He breathed hotly against her ear. "Kuzara, I still can't believe you're mine."

He continued pumping, the nodules along his shaft stimulating her inner walls and bringing her higher and higher. He tilted his hips, and she felt the pressure of his mating rod against her ass, pushing insistently. She gasped as he entered her, the added pressure almost too much, yet making her want more.

Both shafts now entering her, he thrust deeper and deeper, filling her completely. Her inner walls fluttered and clenched around him, wrenching a guttural moan from her throat. Then her orgasm hit her like a tsunami, sweeping her up and shattering her into a million glittering pieces. Zhoel roared, thrusting hard and deep, his hot seed filling her and sending her pleasure spiraling even higher. She dug her fingers into his back, clawing as she tried to anchor herself in the storm of ecstasy.

When she finally drifted back to herself, Zhoel lay above her, kissing her throat and ear gently, the slickness of their skin cooling as they both regained their breath. "My mate," he whispered.

Happy warmth spread through her, a sense of peace and belonging that she'd never felt before. It was as if she could feel Zhoel's very essence, his emotions and thoughts intertwining with her own. It was intimate in a way that went beyond the physical, a merging of their souls. "My mate," she repeated.

She knew, without a doubt, that this was exactly where she was meant to be—by Zhoel's side, exploring the universe and building a life together.

Lila's breath clouded in front of her as she watched her friends and family take seats in front of the decorated gazebo next to Bloomington's gigantic Christmas tree. So many smiling faces surrounded them. Family, friends, and even a few alien visitors who had come to Bloomington and decided to stay. The community had grown so much in the past year, and Lila couldn't help but feel proud of the part she and Zhoel had played in it.

Today was her wedding day, one year to the day since she and Zhoel had decided to embrace their mate bond, and the town had come together to celebrate. Zhoel's and her decision to make Bloomington the corporate headquarters for their intergalactic dating and travel app had breathed new life into the small town. Now, the streets were bustling with visitors from across the galaxy, and local businesses were thriving in ways no one had expected.

Mayor Gunderson was officiating, greeting guests and grinning beneath his Santa hat. He'd wanted to wear an entire Santa suit, but Lila had talked him out of it, compromising with only the classic red and white cap. At least it matched the red poinsettias and holly decorating the aisles and gazebo. A true Christmas wedding.

The music began, and Sara caught Lila's gaze. She looked gorgeous in a long burgundy fur-lined coat that served as her Maid of Honor dress, and seemed happier than she'd been in a long time. The divorce had been difficult, but in the months since, Sara had found a new sense of peace—and possibly even new love, thanks to Zhoel's app.

"Ready?" Sara asked. Lila nodded, and Sara bent to whisper instructions to Josh and Emily before proceeding down the aisle.

Josh stood proudly in his little suit, one hand gripping Emily's while he waited for his mom to reach the gazebo. Then he guided his little sister forward, slowly enough for her to toss the red rose petals from her basket along the way.

The children reached the end, and the music shifted to the bridal waltz. Dad took her arm, his eyes glistening. "Shall we go?" he asked.

Lila nodded, her heart brimming. "I love you, Dad."

"Love you too, Lila."

They stepped out onto the runner spread across the frosty sidewalk. Lila's wedding dress was crafted out of fabric from the planet Alturra, warm enough for the wintery day but sleek enough to make her feel like a princess. The pale material shimmered with an iridescent glow, and the skirt billowed around her like mist. Delicate strands of micro-pearls were woven across the bodice and down the sleeves like captured stars.

Ahead, Zhoel stood waiting in a human tailored suit that highlighted his blue skin. He gave her a soft smile, the warmth of his love resonating through their bond. Tom stood next to him as his Best Man, though her brother still seemed to enjoy giving Zhoel grief about using "alien powers" on his sister.

Mom, Aunt Maggie, and Nana Pearl sat in the front row, all wrapped in thick knitted shawls. Mom was dabbing her eyes but smiling. Nana winked at Lila and said loud enough for everyone to hear, "When you know, you know."

Lila hugged her dad, then turned and stepped up next to Zhoel. Mayor Gunderson smiled at them, his eyes merry as he began to speak. "Dear friends, we are gathered here today to witness and celebrate the union of Lila Carson and Zhoel Aedul."

As the mayor continued with the ceremony, Lila met Zhoel's gaze, filled with love and a promise of forever. Although they'd already been bonded for a year, she still felt almost overwhelmed when she looked at him. She loved her family and had been willing to give up her dreams for them. Now she had everything she could've ever wanted.

"I do," Zhoel said, his voice steady and clear.

Tears prickled the corners of Lila's eyes, and she smiled through them as she said, "I do."

Cheers erupted from the crowd as the mayor declared, "I now pronounce you husband and wife. You may kiss the bride."

Zhoel swept her into his arms, capturing her lips in a passionate kiss. The crowd's cheers filled the air, and Lila laughed, her heart feeling lighter than it had ever been. There were so many adventures still to come—so many places to explore, both on Earth and beyond. And she knew, deep in her heart, that Bloomington would always be a part of those adventures. It was their home base, the place where everything had begun. And with Zhoel's app, there were sure to be more love stories waiting to unfold, stories that would bring even more magic to this small town.

As she and Zhoel walked hand in hand through the cheering crowd, Lila looked up at him and whispered, "Merry Christmas, my love."

Zhoel's eyes shone. "Merry Christmas, Lila. Here's to forever."

At the end of the aisle, they kissed once more, surrounded by the people they loved. This was the happiest Christmas of all—and the future was brighter than Lila had ever imagined.

Dear Reader,

Thank you so much for joining Zhoel on his holiday adventures! This is the first Christmas romance I've ever written, and it was a joy to mix some Kirenai world-building with cozy holiday charm. I hope you had as much fun reading it as I did writing it.

If you'd like more of Zhoel and Lila's story, I'm offering some exclusive deleted scenes just for my VIP Club members! You can read an expanded moment from Zhoel's past, more carnival fun, and an extra heartwarming encounter with Whiskers the cat. Plus, as a VIP member, you'll get a weekly newsletter with sneak peeks of my upcoming books, giveaways, and news about my life in Alaska.

I'd love to have you join the fun! You can sign up and get those scenes here:

https://bit.ly/zhoel-bonus

XOXO, Tamsin

P.S. If you're ready to meet more hot blue shapeshifters like Zhoel, you can buy the entire Kirenai Fated Mates series directly from my store at a great discount. Visit store.tamsinley.com and get the bundle today.

KIRENAI FACT SHEET

**Kirenai** are an all-male species of shapeshifters with a natural form (resting state) like an amoeba who usually assume a bipedal shape to interact with other species. Until the discovery of humans, Kirenai required a permanent pair-bond with a female of another species to produce offspring. All Kirenai traits are dominant and located on the Y chromosome; male offspring are fully Kirenai, while female offspring are fully of the mother's species.

Birth rates have been historically low, and over the ages, the population has dwindled. Human females are exceptionally receptive to impregnation, and do not require formation of a pair-bond to conceive, which has made Earth a target for black market slave traders who deal in "breeders." The Emperor is making attempts to protect the population.

Regardless of the shape a Kirenai's matrix is in, he cannot change his skin or hair color. The most common color is blue, although hues range anywhere from mint green to lavender. Rare individuals, called *burendo,* can vary coloration outside this range. Kirenai blood is clear or slightly milky unless infected, when it grows murky to almost solid white.

All Kirenai have empathic abilities called *Iki'i* which make them capable of reading emotion and desire, and also enables them to identify individuals within their own species regardless of shape. This is the only Kirenai trait sometimes passed on to female progeny. The ability also makes the species consummate lovers because they can take actions and form attributes their partner finds most appealing. Bonded mates assume a permanent form pleasing to their mates; rarely can they force themselves into an alternate shape after bonding.

The average Kirenai life-span is approximately eight hundred human years. When a pair-bond is formed, a Kirenai passes a small genetic market to his mate that mitigates the aging process, giving the mate a lifespan to match his own.

**Khargal** – A horned, gray-skinned race that can enter a hybernating state where their body becomes stonelike. The number of horns indicates the amount of royal blood in them. Honor is more important to them than anything. They have wings and claws and resemble gargoyles of Earth mythology. Their planet of origin is a barren world that has two moons and is known for having some unusual ore deposits and relatively few life forms.

**Fogarian** – A burly, thick-skinned race with crimson hair, claws, and fangs. They come from a high-gravity planet rich in crystalline gemstones and excel at digging. The females usually bear litters of two to four offspring, and are favored mates for Kirenai. Fogarians tend to be very straightforward and keep their promises, even if it means death.

**Vatosangan** – A small, slight race with alabaster skin, rounded features, and blue to black hair. As the most common race to pair-bond with Kirenai, some say they actually control the galactic empire behind the scenes. They seek any alliance, technology, or advantage that will benefit them, and their current government is a meritocracy.

**Human** – New members the Galactic Consortium. This bipedal race has not yet homogenized into a single language, culture or appearance. The species has skin tones that vary between black and alabaster, with shades of brown in between. The females are capable of reproducing with many other species throughout the galaxy, and have become a target for illegal slave trading.

**Qalqan** – A pink, lizard-like race who are innately skilled at medicine. They have more than two genders and change genders as they age, which makes reproduction rather complex. It also means means they rarely pair-bond with Kirenai. In addition, their emotions are hard to understand for others and unreadable by Kirenai *iki'i*.

**Hypawa** – A race with large, expressive eyes, smooth luminescent skin, and luscious hair on their heads and eyelashes; considered by many to be the most beautiful race in the galaxy. Their origin is a mystery - even their supposed world of origin doesn't seem to be their homeworld. Their economy is dependent on tourism and entertainment.

**G'nax** – A spiny, bug-like race that can breathe a variety of atmospheres. Biologically they are inclined to be traders and have senses that let them navigate through hyperspace. They use light to communicate attraction and arousal. The females have a symbiotic relationship with an eight-legged insectoid which secretes dew used to feed G'naxian infants.

**Klen** – A green-skinned humanoid race with eyes on extendable stalks. Their tongues can act as prehensile limbs, and they have the ability to withstand a wide range of temperatures. They are a race of scavengers and can modify some of their bodily secretions to become various useful substances.

**Hage** – Short, bald, gray-skinned aliens with large heads. They were the first to make contact with humans. Though their scrawny frame doesn't suggest it, they are addicted to the pleasures of taking nutrition, and their cuisine is spectacular. A past war obliterated their homeworld, and they now live scattered among the other races, usually employed in a service capacity.

**Sheeghr** – Not advanced enough to be admitted to the Galactic Consortium. A matriarchal, ferret-like race native to the Singing Planet. Known for hypersexuality, the females maintain a constant state of pregnancy to ward off a native parasite called a Gloor. Any female who refuses or who cannot get pregnant is killed. The males determine rank based on the size and color of their phalluses.

# ABOUT THE AUTHOR

Once upon a time I thought I wanted to be a biomedical engineer, but experimenting on lab rats doesn't always lead to happy endings. Now I blend my nerdy infatuation of science with character-driven romance and guaranteed happily-ever-afters. My monsters always find their mates, with feisty heroines, tortured heroes, and all the steamy trouble they can handle. I promise my stories will never leave you hanging (although you may still crave more!)

When I'm not writing, I'll be in the garden or the kitchen, exploring Alaska with my husband, or preparing for the zombie apocalypse. I also enjoy crocheting while binge watching Netflix, playing video games, and enjoying family time during our weekly D&D session.

Interested in more about me? Join my VIP Club and get free books, notices, and other cool stuff!

www.tamsinley.com

BB bookbub.com/authors/tamsin-ley

g goodreads.com/TamsinLey

f facebook.com/TamsinLey

a amazon.com/author/tamsin